Centenary Collection

**Celebrating 100 years of romance with
the very best of Mills & Boon**

*First published in Great Britain 2008
by Harlequin Mills & Boon Limited,
Eton House, 18-24 Paradise Road, Richmond, Surrey TW9 1SR*

© Helen Bianchin 1998

ISBN: 978 0 263 86624 7

77-0109

Harlequin Mills & Boon policy is to use papers that are natural, renewable and recyclable products and made from wood grown in sustainable forests. The logging and manufacturing processes conform to the legal environmental regulations of the country of origin.

*Printed and bound in Spain
by Litografia Rosés S.A., Barcelona*

The Seduction Season

by
Helen Bianchin

MILLS & BOON®

Pure reading pleasure

Helen Bianchin was born in New Zealand and travelled to Australia before marrying her Italian-born husband. After three years they moved, returned to New Zealand with their daughter, had two son,s then resettled in Australia. Encouraged by friends to recount anecdotes of her years as a tobacco sharefarmer's wife living in an Italian community, Helen began setting words on paper and her first novel was published in 1975. An animal lover, she says her terrier and Persian cat regard her study as much theirs as hers. Helen is one of Mills & Boon® Modern™'s top authors and loved by readers around the world.

CHAPTER ONE

IT WAS neither wise nor sensible to drive for hours through the night without taking a break, but Anneke didn't feel inclined to covet wisdom.

And 'sensible' wasn't a suitable word to apply to someone who, only that morning, had told her boss precisely what she thought of him, then walked out of his office and out of his life.

Men. Anneke swore viciously beneath her breath. Words at which her sweet Aunt Vivienne would have blenched in dismay had she heard them uttered from her favourite niece's lips.

'Oh, darling, *no*,' Aunt Vivienne had responded in genuine empathy to Anneke's call. 'Come and stay with me for a while. The weather is beautiful, and you can relax.'

Family. How wonderfully they rose to the occasion in times of need, Anneke reflected fondly. Especially this particular member, who was surrogate mother, aunt, *friend*.

The small seaside cottage situated on a relatively isolated stretch of beach in northern New South Wales was idyllic, and it had taken Anneke only an hour to make a few essential phone calls before tossing some clothes into a bag. Then she locked her elegant small flat in Sydney's suburban Lane Cove, slid behind the wheel of her car, and headed for the main highway leading north.

'I won't arrive until late,' she'd warned her aunt, who had blithely responded it didn't matter in the least; the front door key would be left in the usual place.

Anneke glanced at the illuminated digital clock on the dashboard. Three minutes past midnight. It would take another hour to reach the outskirts of Byron Bay, a few more minutes to traverse the road leading down to her Aunt's beachside cottage.

It was a dark night, with no moon to cast an opalescent glow over the countryside, and she leaned forward to switch on the air-conditioning in an attempt to sharpen a brain dulled by more than nine hours of driving with only two minimum breaks along the way.

The car's headlights probed the ribbon of asphalt and its grassy fringes, and she held back from increasing speed. A semi-trailer barrelled past her, its rig brightly lit, followed a few minutes later by another. Drivers on a tight schedule hauling freight overnight.

Anneke stifled a yawn, rolled her shoulders, then turned on the radio, scrolling through the stations until she found one providing upbeat music.

It was one o'clock when she reached the familiar turn-off and only minutes before she drew the car to a halt on the grassy verge adjacent her aunt's garage.

The outside light was on in welcome, and Anneke switched off the engine, withdrew her bag from the boot, then trod the path quietly to the front porch, retrieved the key and let herself in.

It was an old brick cottage, renovated over the years to incorporate modern conveniences, and immaculately maintained. Its design was basic, with rooms leading off a wide central hall that ran the length of the cottage. Lounge, dining room and kitchen on the right; three bedrooms, bathroom and laundry on the left.

Anneke shut the front door and locked it, then moved quietly to the rear of the house. She'd deposit her bag in the guest bedroom, then make a much needed cup of tea.

There would, she knew, be a cup and saucer set out on the buffet in readiness, and a small plate of sandwiches beneath film-wrap waiting for her in the refrigerator.

A thoughtful gesture by a very kind lady.

The guest bedroom looked endearingly familiar. A double brass bed occupied centre space, with its old-fashioned white lace bedspread heaped with lace-covered cushions. Above the headboard was a snowy white canopy holding a billowing mosquito net. Superfluous, considering the screened windows, but Aunt Vivienne had wanted to retain the old-fashioned ambience, so the canopy remained.

White lace frilled curtains at the window, old-fashioned wooden furniture, and highly polished wooden floors.

It would be so easy to slip off her shoes, shed her clothes, and sink into bed. For a moment she almost considered it. Her shoulders ached, her head ached, and she was so tired, not to mention emotionally exhausted.

She was inclined to add 'devastated'. Although that wasn't quite the description she wanted. Angry, certainly. With Adam, her boss. And herself. Especially herself, for believing in him. She'd been a fool to think she was different from the steady stream of women who inhabited his life.

The type of man, she reflected viciously, who constantly sought challenges on a professional and personal level,

Adam knew all the right moves, which buttons to press. He was very, very good at setting the seduction scene.

But not quite good enough. She retained a clear image of his surprise when she'd announced her intention of walking out. The practised hurt when she'd refused to accept his assurance *she* was very important to him. The slightly wry smile and the spread of his hands in silent acceptance of her vilification that he'd never change.

The only satisfaction she had…and it was very minor…was the knowledge she'd been the one to end the affair. Something she was sure had never happened to him before.

The bravery had lasted as she'd walked out of his office, and all through the long hours of driving.

Now that she was here, reaction began to set in, and she could feel the prick of angry tears.

A quick shower first, she determined wearily, then she would go into the kitchen.

Five minutes later she emerged from the bathroom wearing an oversize tee-shirt. Her face was scrubbed clean of make-up, and her hair hung loose halfway down her back.

In the bedroom she reached into her bag and extracted a few necessities, then she made her way towards the kitchen.

If she didn't know differently, she would almost swear she could sense the subtle aroma of freshly brewed tea.

A faint frown creased her forehead, and she suffered a pang of guilt. Surely she hadn't disturbed Aunt Vivienne, and the dear woman hadn't risen from her bed to offer tea and comfort at this late hour?

It was typical of her caring aunt, and she summoned a warm smile in welcome as she entered the kitchen.

Only to have the smile freeze on her face as a tall, dark-haired stranger shifted his lengthy frame from a leaning position against the servery.

A very tall man with broad, sculpted features, dark grey eyes, and black hair that fell thickly almost to his shoulders.

Anneke swept him from head to foot in a swift encompassing appraisal, and didn't like what she saw.

He was in need of a shave, and bore what looked like a full day's growth of beard that, combined with his dark eyes and long loose hair, gave him a decidedly devilish look. Add well-washed tight-fitting jeans, a black sweatshirt, and he resembled a man who was the antithesis of 'friend'.

'Who the hell are you?'

Uncertainty, defensiveness, fear. He glimpsed each of them in the fleeting emotions chasing across her expressive features.

He should, he reflected with mild exasperation, have taken the time to shave. And, if he'd had a mind to, he could have bound his hair into its customary ponytail at his nape. Could, perhaps should have changed into casual trousers and a polo shirt.

Except the story had been running hot, and he'd lost track of time as he transposed the images in his head into words on the computer screen.

And he'd promised Vivienne that he'd pop over the minute her niece arrived and explain in person why the cottage was empty.

'I've made some tea,' he indicated in a faintly accented drawl. 'Vivienne said you favour Earl Grey.'

Anneke's eyes narrowed. Vivienne. So he knew her aunt. That meant he wasn't an escapee, a felon, or someone of ill repute. Although, looking at him, she wasn't too sure about amending the last description.

'I locked the front door.' Eyes flashed a fiery emerald, then deepened in wariness. 'How did you get in?'

She was attractive, if you had a penchant for tall, slender, long-haired blondes, he mused. Natural, although these days it was hard to tell without getting intimate. Lovely green eyes, beautiful mouth. He felt something stir, then banked it down. Women could complicate a man's life, and he didn't need the aggravation.

Anneke. Pronounced Ann-eek. Scandinavian mother, English father, no siblings. Twenty-seven, para-legal secretary. Just walked out on a louse.

He took one long look at her, and just knew she'd hate it that Vivienne had confided in him.

'Sebastian.' He leant one hip against the servery, and attempted to keep the amusement out of his voice. He partly lowered his eyelids to diminish the gleaming depths. 'And Vivienne gave me a key.'

For tonight? Or had he possessed a key for a while? Aunt Vivienne and a toyboy? The latter aroused an improbable scenario which she instantly dismissed.

Anneke drew herself up to her full height, unaware that the hem of her tee-shirt rose two inches up her thighs. Her voice rose a fraction. 'Sebastian *who*? And you'd better explain real quick why Aunt Vivienne asked you to come into her house at this ungodly hour.'

Dammit, was she wearing anything beneath that thing? Definitely not a bra. Briefs? If she lifted her shoulders much higher he was sure going to find out.

And precisely what, he mused tolerantly, did she think she could do to defend herself against him that he couldn't counteract and deal with before she'd even moved an inch? Kick-boxing, karate? He was trained and adept in each.

'Lanier,' he responded indolently.

So he was French. That explained the slight accent.

'Friend and neighbour.' One eyebrow slanted, and his mouth tilted fractionally. 'Requested by Vivienne to tell you in person news she felt would be too stark if penned in a written note left for you to read in the early-morning hours.'

Anneke was trying hard to retain a hold on her composure. 'So on the basis of good neighbourly relations you came over here at—' she paused to check her watch '—one-thirty in the morning, made me a cup of tea, and waited to tell me-*what*?'

'You're a mite ungrateful.'

His slow drawl held a degree of cynical humour, and it made her want to throw something at him. Surely would have if the sudden sharpness in those dark eyes and the subtle reassemblage of facial muscle hadn't warned her it would be infinitely wise not to follow thought with action.

'I've been on the road for eleven hours.' Her body stance changed, became more aggressive. 'I let myself in to my aunt's cottage and discover a strange, disreputable man calmly making himself at home in her kitchen, and I'm expected to smile and say, *Hi, my name is Anneke, what's yours? How nice, you've made some tea*?'

'And impolite,' he continued, as if she hadn't spoken at all.

'What do you object to? The "disreputable" tag?' Her eyes raked his lengthy frame, skimmed over broad shoulders, muscled chest, narrow hips, long, muscular legs, then slid back to his face. 'Sorry, Sebastian.' She gave his name faint emphasis. 'From where I'm standing, you hardly represent a trustworthy image.'

The eyes lost their tinge of amusement and acquired a

perceptive hardness that changed his persona into something dangerous.

He watched those splendid emerald depths dilate, and felt a moment's satisfaction. 'Vivienne is in Cairns.' The unadulterated facts. He gave them to her without redress. 'She had a call an hour after yours to say her daughter had gone into labour six weeks early. She caught the late-afternoon flight out of Coolangatta.'

Colour drained from her face. Elise was expecting a second set of twins. Six weeks premature. 'How is she?' The words whispered from her lips.

His eyes narrowed faintly. So she cared. Deeply. That was something. 'Vivienne said she'll ring early morning with an update.'

The exhaustion seemed more marked, the faint smudges beneath her eyes a little darker. She looked, he decided, as if she should sit down. He crossed to the small kitchen table and pulled out a chair, then transferred the cup and saucer from the buffet.

'Tea. Hot, white, one sugar.'

Just the way she liked it. Anneke owed thanks to her aunt. And an apology to this large, faintly brooding stranger.

Neighbour? There was only one cottage in close proximity, and that was owned, according to Aunt Vivienne, by a lovely author who kept strange hours. He was also something of a handyman who had, Anneke recalled sketchily from her aunt's correspondence, fixed her roof, replaced a blown fuse, lopped two overgrown trees, and undertaken some heavy garden landscaping.

Anneke regarded the man standing at the table with a faint frown. Not by any stretch of the imagination could she call him 'lovely'.

Mid to late thirties. Ruggedly attractive in a dangerous sort of way, with the type of physical frame that seamlessly melded honed muscle and leashed power together to present a formidable whole.

Let loose, he'd present a ruthless force no man in his right mind would choose to oppose. The woman, she perceived, who willingly stepped into his space would never be sure whether she'd dice with the devil in hell, or soar to heaven with a tutelary saint.

'Are you done?'

Anneke's lashes swept high at his quizzical query, but there was no confusion apparent, no embarrassment. Just analytical regard.

OK, so men weren't her favourite flavour of the month. Justifiable, according to Vivienne, whom he'd driven at speed to the airport that afternoon. *'Such a dear girl.'*

Familial beneficence tended to be biased, he mused. 'Dear' she might be…as a niece, a cousin, a friend. But the woman who stood before him was cool, very cool. With fire beneath the icy façade. He had a very strong desire to stoke the fire and watch the ice melt.

'It was kind of you to carry out my aunt's wishes,' Anneke said formally. It was the closest she intended to get to an apology.

Sebastian inclined his head in mocking acknowledgment. Given the circumstances, and the late hour, he should simply wish her goodnight and leave.

'I'll make fresh tea.' Suiting words to action, he easily dispensed with the cup's contents, flicked the kettle to reboil, and took another teabag from a glass container.

Damn him, did she have to spell it out? 'I'm quite

capable of making it myself.' She crossed to the refrigerator and extracted milk, then took it to the servery.

Big mistake. For it brought her within a hair's breadth of a hard male frame that seemed disinclined to move. Something that tripped the trigger on all her banked-up anger.

The silent rage she'd managed to contain all day burst free. 'You've more than done your good deed for the day.' Fine fury lent her eyes a fiery sparkle, and her knuckles shone white as she clenched her fists. 'I owe you one.'

He looked at her carefully, noted the thinly veiled anger, the exhaustion. 'So please leave?'

'Yes.' Succinct, with an edge of sarcasm.

'Gladly,' he intoned in a dangerously silky voice.

Something shifted in those dark eyes that she didn't want to define, and there was nothing she could do to avoid the firm hands which cupped her face, or prevent the descent of his head as he fastened his mouth over hers.

It was a hard kiss, invasive, with erotic power and a sweet sorcery that took what she refused to give.

No other part of his body touched hers, and he fought against leaning in and gathering her close.

A spark ignited deep inside and flared sharply to brilliant flame. For both of them. He could feel her initial spontaneous response before she refuted it. Sense her surprise, along with his own.

He softened his mouth, took one last tantalising sweep with his tongue, then slowly raised his head.

She looked-*shattered*. Although she recovered quickly.

He smiled, a slow, wide curving of his mouth as he regarded her stormy features, and he dropped his hands from her face. 'Now we're even.'

Then he turned and walked from the kitchen, trod a

path down the hall to the front door, then quietly closed it behind him.

It irked Anneke dreadfully that a few seconds of stunned surprise had rendered her immobile and robbed her of the opportunity to hurl something at him, preferably hard enough to do damage to any part of his anatomy.

Dulled reflex action, brought on by a degree of emotional, mental and physical exhaustion. Something that a good night's rest would do much to rectify, she perceived as she set the kettle to boil again and made fresh tea.

Men, she brooded as she sipped the delicious brew, were arrogant, heartless, self-oriented, entirely governed by their libido, and not worth a minute of her time.

A thought which persisted as she finished her tea, then she crossed to the bedroom and slid in between crisp, clean white sheets.

On the edge of sleep, one image invaded her mind, and it wasn't the sleekly groomed city lawyer in his three-piece business suit.

CHAPTER TWO

HAMMERING noises in close proximity were not conducive to restful slumber.

Anneke heard them in the depths of her subconscious mind and slowly drifted into wakefulness. Still the noise persisted.

What the hell...? She opened one eye and looked at the clock atop the bedside pedestal. Dammit, it was only *seven*. On Saturday.

Surely her aunt hadn't arranged for a contractor to do some work and forgotten to mention the fact?

Maybe if she buried her head beneath the pillow she could go back to sleep, she decided, suiting thought to action, only to groan out loud minutes later as the sound still penetrated with no seeming loss of intensity.

Annoyance had her sliding out of bed and pulling on a pair of shorts, and she paused briefly to drag a brush through the length of her hair before storming into the hall to assess where the hammering seemed loudest.

Rear, she decided, and made for the back door.

Quite what she'd expected to see when she opened it she wasn't sure. Certainly not Sebastian Lanier's tall, broad-shouldered, lean-hipped, jean-clad frame perched part-way up a ladder, wielding a hammer as he stroked in one nail after another.

'Just what the hell do you think you're doing?'

Well, now, there was a pretty sight to tempt a man's eye at this early hour. Nice legs. He followed the slender calves, the well-shaped thighs. Good muscle tone, he noted approvingly.

Narrow hips, neat waist, and the slight swing of her breasts made him itch to slide his hands beneath the oversize tee-shirt and see how well they fit his palms.

Slowly he lifted his eyes and took his time examining her mouth, and remembered the feel of it beneath his own.

He moved up a few inches and looked straight into a pair of bright, furious eyes whose emerald depths threatened nothing less than murder.

Sebastian smiled. A long, slow, curving movement that lifted the edges of his mouth and showed the gleam of white teeth. 'Good morning.' He positioned another nail and hammered it in.

Clean-shaven, his hair bound neatly at his nape, he looked almost respectable. It was the 'almost' part she had trouble coming to terms with. None of the men in the circles in which she moved resembled anything like *this* man.

Calm, she must remain calm. 'Do you know what time it is?'

Of course he knew what time it was. He'd been up since six, had orange juice, gone through his daily exercise routine, then assembled a high-protein drink in the blender and sipped it while he scrolled through his e-mail.

'Am I disturbing you?'

Oh, he was disturbing her, all right. Just how much, he was about to discover. A last attempt at civility, then she'd let him have it with both barrels blazing. 'Perhaps you'd care to explain what exactly it is that you're doing?'

She possessed a fine temper. He could see it in her eyes, the tilt of her chin, the way she stood.

'Yesterday I removed a section of worn guttering. Today I'm putting up new.' He held another nail in position and nailed it in. Then he turned his head to look at her. 'I arranged it with Vivienne.'

There was that faint smile again. Anneke gritted her teeth.

He moved down the ladder and shifted it, checked its stability, then stepped up again. And hammered in another nail.

'I suppose you're one of those irritating people who manage to get by on an indecently few hours of sleep?'

'Five or six.' He lined up another nail and rammed it home.

Anger coursed through her body, heating her veins, and erupted in voluble speech. 'You're doing this deliberately, aren't you?'

He cast her a long, measured glance, noted the twin flags of colour high on each cheek, the firm set of her mouth. 'Is that an accusation?'

'Damned right it is,' she bit out furiously.

Sebastian hooked the hammer into his toolbelt and descended down to the ground. 'Let's get one thing clear. I boot up my computer at one in the afternoon. Vivienne needs something fixed; I fix it for her. In the morning.'

His voice was quiet, almost too quiet. And silky, she decided. 'You have to start at *seven*?'

'I'm due in town at ten,' he explained reasonably. 'I won't have time to do anything when I get back from town except grab some lunch, and—''

'Go boot up the computer,' Anneke finished for him. 'And you just had to finish this section before you left.'

'Yes.'

'Today.'

'It could rain,' he responded solemnly.

Most unlikely. Her voice rose a pitch. 'You waltz over here and begin hammering shortly after dawn?'

'Dawn was five-thirty, daylight saving time,' Sebastian informed her mildly.

'I don't give a tinker's cuss when dawn was.' She advanced a step, and crossed her arms across her chest. 'I want you to stop hammering so I can get some sleep.'

'Ask me nicely.'

Her jaw went slack. 'I beg your pardon?'

His lips twitched. 'Ask me nicely,' he reiterated.

So he was amused. Well, she'd wipe that smile right off his face! 'You can go—' she enunciated each word carefully '—jump in the ocean.'

The phone rang, its peal issuing an insistent summons she chose to ignore. Temporarily.

'That'll probably be Vivienne.'

It didn't help any that he was right. Elise was stable; the unborn twins were fine. However, Elise would stay in hospital, probably until the twins' birth, anticipated prematurely. Naturally Aunt Vivienne would remain in Cairns.

'I'm so sorry.' The older woman's voice was achingly sincere. 'I feel a little easier in my mind knowing Sebastian is close by.'

A sentiment Anneke didn't share.

'You've met him, of course,' Aunt Vivienne continued. 'Such a thoughtful, caring man. And so handy. Oh, dear, I almost forgot—'" She broke off, paused, then launched into an explanation. 'I have an arrangement to prepare his evening meals. Anneke, could you?' A hesitant apology swiftly followed. 'I hate to ask, but would it be too much of an imposition?'

Yes, it would. If she never saw Sebastian Lanier again, it would be too soon! The thought of preparing a cooked meal for him every night was unbearable.

However, being Aunt Vivienne's guest, enjoying her aunt's home, made it difficult to refuse. 'I'll organise it with him,' she agreed, hiding her reluctance.

'Thank you, darling.' Aunt Vivienne's relief was palpable. 'You're such a good cook, far more adventurous than me. He's in for a gourmet feast.'

The word 'gourmet' struck a responsive chord, and Anneke allowed herself a slight smile. If Aunt Vivienne wanted her to prepare Sebastian's evening meals during her sojourn here, then she would. However, meat-and-potatoes-with-vegetables would definitely be off the menu.

A contemplative gleam entered her eyes. Sautéed brains, stuffed pigeon, pig's trotters. She gave a silent laugh. Maybe this might be fun, after all.

'I'll take care of it, Aunt Vivienne.' Oh, she would, indeed! 'Is there anything else you'd like me to do?'

'No, sweetheart. Thank you. I'll ring again in a day or two, or before if there's any news.'

'Give Elise my love.' Anneke replaced the receiver, and noticed the absence of hammering.

Had Sebastian finished? Or was he merely being courteous? She moved towards the back door and saw his lengthy frame bending over a stack of neatly piled wood.

Nice butt, she acknowledged. Some men looked good in tight, worn denim, and he was one of them. As she watched, he straightened and turned to face her.

'Good news?'

She was on the verge of retorting that it was none of his business, but managed to catch the words in time. 'Elise is stable; the twins are expected to deliver prematurely.'

Succinct, with just a touch of resentment, he mused, wondering how she would react if he took all that fine anger and turned it into passion.

Probably try to hit him. He banked down a silent laugh and deliberately drooped his eyelids so the gleam of humour was successfully hidden. It might even be interesting to allow her to score the slap.

Anneke regarded him through narrowed eyes, unable to read him. And the inability didn't sit well. Usually she had no difficulty in pegging the male species. Smooth, charming, vain, arrogant, superficial, blatant. Whatever the veneer, the motive remained basic.

Yet instinct warned that *this* man didn't run with the pack, and that made him infinitely dangerous.

Damn his imperturbability. She wanted to shake that unruffled calm. 'Is six o'clock convenient for your evening meal?'

One eyebrow slanted, and she could have sworn she glimpsed a gleam of amusement in those dark eyes. 'Vivienne frequently shared dinner with me.'

She drew in a deep breath, then released it slowly. She even managed the semblance of a smile, albeit that it held a degree of cynicism. 'An example I have no intention of following.'

'You have an aversion to friendliness?'

Anneke could feel the anger rise, and didn't try to contain it. 'An aversion to *you*.'

His expression didn't change, although anyone who knew him well could have warned the stillness held ominous implications.

'You don't know me,' Sebastian intoned softly.

'*Believe* I don't want to.'

'Feel free to stow your bag in the boot of the car and drive back to Sydney.' His eyes were level, and resembled obsidian shards. 'The loss of a prepared evening meal won't negate my obligation to complete necessary chores for Vivienne.'

She drew in a deep breath, then released it slowly. She could, she knew, easily do what he suggested. Aunt Vivienne would accept she'd changed her mind, and be concerned about her ambivalence.

Except she didn't want to return to the city. Given a choice, she'd have preferred her aunt's company, her wisdom. And the solitude of a sandy stretch of beach in a gently curving bay where she could walk alone, meditate, and allow fresh emotional scars to heal.

A solitude she wouldn't gain if she went back to her small city apartment. Friends, concerned for her welfare, would ring and try to entice her to join them at any one of several parties, or attend the cinema, the theatre. Suggest lunch or dinner and attempt to play amateur psychologist.

Unburdening her soul and having her every word, every action dissected and analysed didn't form part of her agenda.

'I intend to stay,' Anneke responded with equal civility.

Sebastian hadn't been aware the small knot of tension existed until it suddenly dissolved in his gut. Nor could he explain the reason for its existence.

Sure, Vivienne's niece was a sassy, long-legged blonde whose captivating green eyes invited a second glance.

His mouth formed a slightly bitter twist. He'd known several sassy, long-legged women in his time, and bedded more than a few. Only to discover they'd coveted his wealth first and foremost. With the exception of Yvette, with whom he'd shared one precious year. In an unprecedented twist of fate, she'd been victim of a random road accident on the eve of their wedding.

For two years he'd buried himself in work, diced daringly in the world of high finance, only to wake one morning and opt for a complete change of lifestyle.

He owned apartments, houses, in several major capital cities around the world, and for a while he'd lived in every one of them.

It was in Paris, the country of his birth, where he'd first begun to pen a novel, the idea for which had niggled at his brain for months. The state-of-the-art computer which linked him to his various business interests had acquired a new file.

A file which had grown and totally absorbed him. His path to acceptance and publication had been a dream run. At a time when virtual reality teased the readers' senses, his futuristic upbeat plots had been a hit. International success soon followed, and in a bid for anonymity he'd returned to Australia, sought and found relative isolation in a picturesque bay in the Northern Rivers area, and snapped up a cottage he took pleasure in slowly renovating and refurbishing during the morning hours.

Once a year he flew to the States for the obligatory book launch. And each Christmas was spent in Paris. Occasionally he looked up old friends and joined the social set for a while, only to find the life palled, the new plot beckoned, whereupon he returned to the place he'd called home for the past five years.

Now he looked into the clear green gaze of the first sassy blonde who'd shown an active dislike of him, and relaxed his features as he proffered a faint smile. 'Six o'clock will be fine.'

Where had he been during that long minute of silence? Anneke told herself she wasn't interested. And knew she lied.

She inclined her head stiffly, and matched her voice to the gesture. 'I intend going back to bed.' Her eyes held his, fascinated by dark slate-grey depths whose expression was difficult to discern. 'I'd be grateful if you'd stop hammering so that I can catch up on some sleep.'

'OK.'

She couldn't believe he intended to comply. 'You'll stop?'

Those sensuously moulded lips curved slightly. 'You asked me nicely.'

Anneke opened her mouth, then closed it again.

She watched in silence as he removed the ladder and stored it, gathered up the used section of roof guttering and collected his tools.

Without a further word he turned and covered the distance to his cottage with an easy, lithe stride.

Denim hugged every curve, hinted at superb thigh and calf muscle, and emphasised the length of his legs. Lean waist, fluid muscular grace evident in the breadth of his shoulders denoted more than average strength.

Dammit, why was she standing here *watching* him, for heaven's sake? Men weren't her favoured species at the moment, and *this* man irritated her beyond measure.

She retreated indoors, paused long enough in the

kitchen to fill a glass with water and drink it, then she made for the bedroom and slid between the sheets.

The anger hadn't subsided; if anything it had intensified. Joined by the stinging realisation that she had no job, no salary, and running expenses to maintain on her apartment.

On the plus side, she had an annuity from inherited investments, sufficient to live quite comfortably until she found employment, and there was a reasonably healthy savings account from which she could draw funds to meet weekly expenses.

Anneke closed her eyes and deliberately summoned pleasant thoughts, employed meditation techniques, and resorted to counting sheep. Nothing worked.

With an angry jerk she tossed off the sheet, rose and pulled on a swimsuit. A swim, followed by a walk along the beach, then breakfast. After which she'd examine the contents of Aunt Vivienne's refrigerator and pantry, decide what to prepare for Sebastian's dinner, then drive into Byron Bay and collect everything she needed from the supermarket.

Anneke paused long enough to clean her teeth and run a brush through her hair, then she slid on a pair of sunglasses, caught up a towel, and made her way down onto the sandy foreshore.

The sun was warm, with the promise of increasing heat as the day progressed. A faint sea breeze teased the ends of her hair, and she inhaled the tangy salt air with pleasure.

There wasn't another person in sight, and she relished the solitude, choosing to explore the familiar shoreline for several minutes before opting to wade into the cool water.

Effecting a neat dive, she broke the surface and began a pattern of leisurely strokes parallel to the shore for a while, before emerging to towel the excess moisture from her skin and hair.

It didn't take long for the warm air to dry her swimsuit, and she wrapped the towel round her waist, then set out towards the outcrop of rocks at the furthest end of the bay.

Anneke could feel her body relax as the tension eased, and she increased her pace to a light jog, enjoying the exercise, the morning, the solitude.

It was almost an hour before she re-entered the cottage, and after a shower she dressed in casual shorts and a top, then caught up a pad and pen as she examined her aunt's pantry and refrigerator and noted what food supplies she'd need to collect from the supermarket.

CHAPTER THREE

BREAKFAST comprised cereal, toast and fruit, followed by ruinously strong black coffee.

Anneke tidied the few dishes, then she caught up her car keys, slid the strap of her bag over one shoulder, and made her way out to the carport.

Byron Bay was a pleasant seaside town, a popular holiday area, and the community centre for outlying banana, avocado and sugar cane farmers.

Parking the car wasn't a problem, and she took her time browsing through the supermarket as she selected her purchases and stacked them in the trolley.

It was almost midday when she returned to the cottage, and after unloading her various purchases she took time to have lunch before beginning preparations for Sebastian's evening meal.

At five she showered and changed into jeans and a singlet top, bound her hair into a single plait, then returned to the kitchen.

Artichokes stuffed and served with a rich cream sauce, marinated baby octopus, *risi e bisi*, two baby pigeons *confits aux raisins*, and, for dessert, her speciality—*bombe au chocolat*.

Anneke hoped he had a supply of antacid on hand, otherwise he was certain to be a victim of indigestion.

At precisely two minutes before six she trod the short path linking both cottages and knocked on Sebastian's back door.

She heard a deep bark, followed by a curt command, then the door swung open.

Anneke saw the dog first. A huge Alsatian with liquid brown eyes, a dark velvet pelt, and possessing all the qualities of a trained guard dog.

'Shaef,' Sebastian qualified. 'Let him become acquainted, then you'll never need worry about him again.'

Her eyes travelled over snug black jeans, a black open-necked shirt, to features that bore a faintly mocking expression.

He was an arresting man, compelling, and possessed of a leashed quality that some would find vaguely frightening.

Anneke didn't question his authority with Shaef. She had a healthy respect for canines, and the Alsatian was an awesome breed.

'Will you come in?'

'No,' she responded quickly. Too quickly, for she saw the sudden gleam apparent in his eyes, and caught the slight quirk at the edge of his mouth. 'Enjoy your meal.'

'Merci.'

No man had the right to look so darned sexy, or possess a voice that sounded like melted chocolate being dribbled over ice cream. Smooth, very smooth, she perceived. Yet there was tensile steel beneath the smoothness. The hardness of a man well-versed in the frailties of his fellow men.

Without a further word she turned and retraced her steps. In her aunt's kitchen she set about cleaning up, then when it was done she made herself a light, fluffy omelette, added a salad, and took the plate into the dining room.

Tomorrow night she'd serve him everything stuffed... carpet steak with an exotic sauce, stuffed mushrooms, zucchini, tomatoes and potatoes. She would even bake a vanilla sponge for dessert and stuff it with fresh strawberries and cream whipped with kirsch.

And Monday... She positively *glowed* at the thought of what she could do with seafood.

Anneke prayed fervently that if he didn't already have an ulcer, her epicurean offerings would soon provide him with one. Revenge, she determined, would be sweet.

Very sweet, she determined, upon waking next morning to the shrilling sound of an electric skill-saw cutting through wood.

Anneke spared a glance at her watch. Six-thirty. A half-hour earlier than yesterday. At least this morning she wasn't the victim of only a few hours' sleep.

If Sebastian Lanier was playing a game, then so, too, would she.

A slight smile played over her lips and she slid from the bed. A visit to the bathroom, then she pulled on briefs, shorts, and a singlet top. Her hair she deftly twisted into a single braid and let it fall between her shoulders. Then she slipped her feet into joggers and went to the back door with a ready smile in place.

He wore the same faded stonewashed jeans from the day before, and a different tee-shirt. Nice muscle structure, tight butt, firm waist, with no visible fat apparent on that mean frame.

'Good morning,' she greeted as she ran lightly down the

few steps. 'I had no idea Aunt Vivienne needed more repairs. What is it today?'

He pulled the switch on the electric saw and straight-ened as he turned to face her. The dark hair was neatly bound, but he had forgone the morning shave. It gave him a distinctly piratical look, and heightened the planes of his face, sculpted hard cheekbones and emphasised the strength of his jaw.

If he'd suffered a restless night due to indigestion, it didn't show.

'A section of the picket fence needs replacing. New posts, new palings.'

She widened the smile, and her eyes took on a sparkling gleam. 'How kind. Aunt Vivienne will be pleased.' She turned towards the path leading down to the beach, then cast him a backward glance over one shoulder. 'Have a nice day.'

Anneke broke into a leisurely jog, and on reaching the sand she crossed down to the water's edge and ran parallel to the shoreline until she reached the outward curve of the bay, then she slowed to a halt and went through her usual morning exercise routine.

She deliberately took her time, and when she returned to the cottage Sebastian was nowhere in sight. The carpen-ter's horse, any wood cut-offs had been cleared away, and a brief glance along the length of picket fence displayed the new section in place.

A muted throaty purr from an engine sounded loud in the morning's silence, and she turned towards its source. Reversing from Sebastian's garage was a late model Range Rover, with, she soon saw, Sebastian at the wheel.

So he was going out. Good, she thought happily as she let herself into the cottage. She had a few household chores to perform, then she'd shower and put a call through to Aunt Vivienne. After lunch she intended to curl up in a comfortable chair and read until it was time to begin preparing Sebastian's dinner.

Anneke had just finished lunch when the phone rang, and she crossed the room and lifted the receiver from its handset.

Her usual cheery greeting brought no response, so she repeated it. Still nothing. She was about to hang up when she heard the soft sound of human breathing.

Even, steady, it became louder and faster, until there could be no mistaking the implied simulation.

She cut the connection in one quick movement, then stood transfixed for several seconds before shaking herself free from momentary shock.

It was simply a random call, she attempted to rationalise. Perhaps some kid with too much time on his hands was getting his kicks from indiscriminate dialling.

Yet it gave her an eerie feeling, one that was difficult to dispel as she tried valiantly to lose herself in the plot of the current mystery she was reading.

Preparations for Sebastian's dinner didn't take overlong, and at a few minutes to six she took the loaded tray and carried it across to his cottage.

Sebastian appeared at the door seconds after she knocked. A white tee-shirt was teamed with black jeans, and both fitted snug on his frame.

He surveyed her with interest, caught the seemingly pleasant smile, and wasn't deceived.

His gaze flicked to the tray in her hand, and he didn't know whether to castigate or commend her.

Much depended on whether last night's meal had been a one-off, or if she'd duplicated dishes of which, while each separate one was a gourmet delight, the combination left something to be desired.

He thought of the rich *bombe au chocolat* reposing on a shelf in his refrigerator. Death by chocolate? Somehow he had the feeling the dessert was meant to be his *bête noir*.

'Enjoy.'

'Thank you,' Sebastian acknowledged as he took the tray, watching as she took a few seconds to fondle Shaef's ears. Then she turned towards Vivienne's cottage, and he viewed the elegant sway of her hips with male appreciation before taking the tray to the dining room table.

Shaef cast him an enquiring look and pricked his ears.

'That makes two of us,' Sebastian murmured as he placed dishes onto the table, caught up cutlery, and removed covers.

It only took a glance to interpret Anneke's meaning. Get stuffed. A slow, musing smile widened his mouth.

Vivienne's niece had gone to considerable trouble to exact revenge.

With deft movements he consigned the sponge, strawberries and cream concoction to the refrigerator.

Pride had prevented her from serving up burnt offerings, or the blandest of fare. Pride, and loyalty to her aunt.

Well, he wouldn't spoil Anneke's game.

He, too, could employ a little subterfuge. If most all of the minor repairs around Vivienne's property were completed within a week instead of the months she'd originally suggested, then so be it.

A slow smile curved his mouth, and the edges lifted in humour. And if he ran out of things to do, then he would invent some.

Sebastian sat down at the table and carefully removed

a portion of stuffing from each vegetable, then sliced into the delectable-looking steak.

A man would need to be wary around a woman like Anneke. His lips twitched and his eyes gleamed with cynical amusement. If each prepared meal provided an indication of her mood, then the next week or two could prove interesting.

Afterwards he scraped discarded stuffing into the refuse bin, made recklessly strong coffee, then carried it through to the office, turned on the computer screen and began to work.

Intrigued to discover within a short space of time that a minor female character of his creation had developed a few traits that changed stoic to sassy.

Anneke surveyed the number of pots and kitchen utensils atop the kitchen benchtop and wrinkled her nose at the folly of creating culinary mayhem.

Rinse and soak, she decided, then she'd attack the dishes when she'd eaten her own modest meal of salad greens with nuts, fresh cantaloupe, mango and feta cheese.

Afterwards, she'd thumb through Aunt Vivienne's numerous cookbooks and plot a menu for tomorrow evening's meal, then list the ingredients she needed to buy.

At nine Aunt Vivienne rang, with an update on Elise's health and the latest monitor results on the unborn twins. It was a case of 'no change' being good news.

Almost as soon as Anneke replaced the receiver, her mobile phone rang, and she indulged in a lengthy chat with a friend in Sydney before ending the call and retiring to bed with a book.

The morning brought a light rain, and after a leisurely breakfast Anneke showered and changed, then drove to Byron Bay to collect fresh seafood.

On impulse she opted to spend the day baking, and purchased ingredients to make a Christmas cake. Several small ones, she decided, would make excellent gifts for friends, wrapped in red and green Cellophane and tied with decorative ribbons. She could take them back with her, or, if she chose to lengthen her stay, then she could consign them via the postal service.

It rained on and off all day. Alternate heavy and light showers with very little time in between.

The kitchen was soon redolent with various aromas, as Anneke washed and soaked a variety of dried fruit in sherry and brandy.

By mid-afternoon shortbread, cut in fingers, lay cooling on baking racks. There was one tin filled with rumballs, another with fudge brownies. Tomorrow she'd bake Christmas cakes.

A quick glance at her watch determined it was time to begin preparing Sebastian's evening meal.

A secretive smile teased the edges of her mouth. She almost wished she could see his expression when he uncovered a platter containing miso soup thick with seaweed and tofu, grilled eel in a rich oyster sauce, sushi with slices of raw fish and seaweed delicacies, and *faux* caviare. Flavoured tofu with fruit comprised dessert.

Sebastian heeded her knock, caught her carefully composed expression, and was immediately on guard.

He mentally conjured the thick T-bone steak he'd removed from the freezer earlier in the day, the makings for a salad he could put together in minutes, and sought to protect his palate.

'Why not join me tomorrow night?'

'I wouldn't dream of interrupting your work,' she responded with extreme politeness.

'An hour or two won't cause much damage.'

'Damage' was the operative word, and she didn't covet an hour in his company, much less two. Besides, if she shared a meal with him she'd have to resort to conventional cooking, and that would definitely spoil the fun.

'Maybe another time.' Without a further word she turned and retraced her steps.

It was as well he liked Japanese food, although he conceded her choice of dishes was probably as deliberate as it was unusual. The dessert joined the chocolate *bombe* and the strawberry sponge sitting in his refrigerator.

Anneke checked the dried fruit, stacked shortbread into one of her aunt's cake tins, then cleaned up the kitchen.

After a day of preparing food, she opted for something simple for her own meal, and followed it with a bowl of fresh fruit. She added ice to a glass, filled it with water, then carried it through to the lounge and switched on the television.

The phone rang at nine. She remembered the time, as she glanced at her watch. Even as she picked up the receiver she had the instinctive feeling this was going to be a repeat of yesterday's nuisance call.

Bingo, Anneke registered as no one answered her greeting, and within seconds she could hear audible breathing on the line.

Who would do something like this? It couldn't be aimed at Aunt Vivienne, surely? Yet who knew Anneke was here?

She cut the connection and replaced the handset, then stood staring at the telephone as if willing it to divulge relevant information.

For five minutes she hovered in the kitchen, wiping down bench surfaces that had already been wiped, checking cupboards, the refrigerator, the pantry. Just in case the call was repeated.

The thought crossed her mind that perhaps she should report it. But what could the police do, except relay advice she was already aware of?

CHAPTER FOUR

SEVERAL friends were aware of Anneke's mobile listing, but she hadn't told anyone of her whereabouts or given out Aunt Vivienne's number. And no one she knew would make a nuisance, heavy breathing, non-speaking call then hang up.

She had no enemies, and no one she knew would wish her harm. So *who*? A frown creased her forehead. A mis-dialled number? Once, maybe. But *twice* indicated it to be premeditated.

The microwave digital display indicated a few minutes before six. Damn. There was no reason to front the day at such an early hour, and yet she felt too unsettled to simply sit around and do nothing.

A jog along the length of the beach followed by a swim in the cool, clear ocean would clear her mind, then she'd drive into Byron Bay and explore the shops for an hour or two. After lunch she'd mix the Christmas cakes and consign them into the oven.

This early there was a fresh newness to the day, apparent in the warmth of the sun's rays, the golden sand crisp from its tidal cleanse.

Anneke set a leisurely pace along the Bay's gentle curve to the outcrop of rocks before turning to retrace her steps.

It was then she saw a lone male figure closing the distance between them, his pace measuring hers in relaxed style but covering the sand more quickly due to a longer stride.

There was no disguising the tall, muscular frame, and if there was any doubt the dark hair sleekly bound at his nape provided recognition.

Sebastian.

Clad in dark sweat-shorts and singlet, he looked like something out of a health and fitness magazine. The sweatband round his head lent a credible likeness to an Apache brave.

The mental switch in image brought a smile to her lips and lit her eyes with a mischievous sparkle.

She watched with detached admiration as he drew close: the fluid flex of well-honed muscle and sinew, the lithe, animalistic grace of perfectly co-ordinated body movement.

At this stage most men would have bunched up their pectoral muscles, flung back their shoulders in an effort to impress a female of the species.

Sebastian merely slowed his stride and came to an easy halt. Lacking was the expected sheen of sweat; nor was there any evidence of shortness of breath.

'Bonjour.'

'Hi.'

The easy smile deepened the vertical crease in each cheek, and there was an appreciative gleam in those dark eyes.

'I didn't expect to see you out this early.'

Dammit, why did it take one glance at his mouth to bring vividly to mind how it felt to have it cover her own? And *why*, a silent voice taunted, should some internal flame ignite and flare into deep, pulsing life with anticipation that it might?

'I rarely sleep in.' She hadn't meant to sound defensive.

Touchy. Definitely touchy. And he wondered why. 'I wasn't aware I'd implied that you do,' he said quietly.

Oh, hell. She had the distinct feeling he could see inside her mind, and meaningful conversation at this hour of the morning wasn't her intention.

'Must keep the heart-rate up,' she indicated, preparing to sprint away from him.

'We could run together.'

'Sorry,' Anneke declared without compunction. 'I run for fun. You,' she said with certainty, 'adhere to a more professional pace.' She even summoned a slight smile. 'And I wouldn't suggest you alter it solely for my benefit.' She broke into a light sprint, then slowed her pace when she had put some distance between them.

It wasn't easy to ignore the faint prickle of awareness teasing the hairs on her nape.

His very presence irked her. He made her feel vulnerable, and she didn't like it any more than she liked him.

There were no messages on the answering machine, but her mobile showed one missed call, and when she checked voice mail all she heard was an indistinct whisper followed by the silent click of a replaced receiver.

Her stomach gave a small lurch, then settled.

Adam? Even as the thought intruded, she dismissed it. Adam Lloyd Chambers was a legal eagle of impeccable lineage, admired by his associates and a pillar within his social community.

The fact he had a penchant for sexual dalliances didn't alter the fact he was an unlikely candidate to make nuisance calls. Besides, she couldn't see him doing anything to jeopardise his career or his partnership.

Anneke made for the bathroom, showered and washed

her hair, then dressed in tailored shorts, added a cotton top.
She cut up a selection of fruit, added cereal, then followed
it with a poached egg on toast for breakfast.

She put a small load of washing through the machine,
and after completing some essential housework she caught
up her keys and drove into Byron Bay with the intention
of browsing through the many craft shops, maybe taking
time out to sip a cappuccino at one of several outdoor cafés
before purchasing a selection of fresh fruit and a few staple
vegetables.

The aroma of freshly baked bread was irresistible, and
she entered the shop, purchased a baguette and a few
savoury scrolls, then emerged out onto the pavement.

Some ham, a wedge of Brie, and a delicious salad would
suffice as lunch. Then she'd curl up in the capacious cane
chair on her aunt's porch and lose herself in a book until
it was time to prepare dinner.

'Well, now, girl, what's that you've got there?'

She heard the voice, took in the thin face, the long,
unkempt hair, the nose-stud, the eyebrow-ring, and a range
of studs and earrings attached to each ear. The loose-
flowing shirt looked as if it hadn't been washed in weeks,
likewise the frayed and slashed jeans.

One glance at those eyes was enough for her to deter-
mine this was no peace-loving New Age devotee. They
were dark, beady, and mean.

Trouble. Unless she handled him carefully.

Anneke lifted one shoulder in a careless shrug. 'Bread,
fruit and vegetables.' She made to move past him, and saw
the subtle shift of his body as he stepped close.

Damn. 'You're in my way,' she stated calmly.

'That's a problem?'

'It could be.'

'So, what you gonna do, pretty girl?' he mocked.

'Any one of a number of things.'

He leered at her, and ran the tip of his tongue over his lower lip. 'Such as?' His mouth parted in a soundless laugh. 'Scream?'

'How's your pain level?' Anneke countered matter-of-factly.

An arm curved along the back of her waist while another deftly removed a carry-bag. '*Chérie.* My apologies.' She felt the heat of Sebastian's frame as he leaned in close and brushed his lips to her cheek in a warm caress. 'Have you been waiting long?'

She turned her head and met a pair of steady dark eyes, glimpsed their warning flare, and controlled the unexpected flip her stomach executed as she became lost in the devastating warmth of his smile.

Only a fool would have ignored the hard-muscled body beneath the open-necked shirt and stonewashed jeans, or dismissed the ruthless intensity behind his deceptively mild expression.

Anneke had the distinct feeling he was poised for action. It was evident in his stance, the sharp stillness apparent in his eyes. For one infinitesimal second she almost felt sorry for her aggressor.

'Sebastian. *C'est opportun.*'

A split second to think. So, not fluent, he acknowledged. The accent was passable. His smile widened. Good. She would understand what he said when he made love to her.

His eyes were carefully bland. 'Should we effect an introduction?' He thrust out his hand and enclosed the young man's palm in a firm grip. 'Lanier. And you?'

'Go to hell.'

Sebastian's expression didn't change. 'What a shame, my friend,' he intoned with deadly softness. 'We're not going there.'

Anneke didn't blink at the blistering and very pithy response. 'Charming,' she murmured facetiously as her aggressor turned and ambled off along the pavement. 'Pity his suggestion was anatomically impossible.'

Sebastian's eyes narrowed fractionally. 'He intended to relieve you of whatever money you had in your wallet.' To fund the next fix.

'It would have been interesting to discover his threshold of pain.'

He cast her a sharp glance. 'What particular method did you have in mind?'

She told him, concisely, analytically, and had the satisfaction of evidencing a measure of respect.

'Reassuring,' he conceded, 'to learn you can take care of yourself.'

Anneke inclined her head. Dealing with the scruffy young creep wouldn't have posed a problem. However, she would have had to discard the carry-bags in a hurry, and to have her carefully selected purchases crushed or broken in a physical fracas would have been a terrible waste.

She turned towards him and raised an enquiring eyebrow. 'And your field of expertise?'

He had trained beneath a well-respected master, practised in many a *dojo*, and occasionally fought in places no civilised self-respecting person would consider while serving his country for a time.

It was simpler to name one. 'Karate.'

Anneke considered him thoughtfully. Most men would

have launched into a string of achievements. However, Sebastian Lanier was not 'most men', and his simplicity intrigued her.

There was more to him than met the eye, she perceived. Entrepreneur, writer. What other vocation and skill did he possess?

Sebastian indicated the carry-bags. 'Anything likely to spoil in there for the next hour?'

'No. Why?'

He deftly turned her in the opposite direction. 'You can join me for lunch.'

She regarded him solemnly. 'It's polite to ask.'

His mouth curved to form a wolfish smile, and there was a gleam in those dark eyes she didn't quite trust. 'I feel it's the least I can do in light of the gastronomic feasts you've prepared for me over the past few nights.'

'Gastronomic' indeed. 'Feast' depended entirely on the interpretation, she decided with irreverent suspicion. 'Thank you.'

There were any number of cafés and restaurants from which to choose. Instead, he led her into a modern pub, the owner of which had gained recognition in the area for his brush with fame and the garnering of considerable wealth. A man's man, and one of the boys, local legend had it, who could sup beer at the bar with his friends equally as well as he'd cemented business deals in Hollywood and London.

'You don't object to a counter lunch?'

She searched Sebastian's features in an attempt to discern whether his choice was deliberate, and found nothing to indicate that it might be.

'It's ages since I had fish and chips.'

He cast her a musing glance. 'I think you'll find they manage something less basic.'

They did, and, although relatively simple fare, the freshly caught grilled schnapper was delicious, the salad superb, and it was obvious the licensee patronised the local bakery.

Sebastian noted her enjoyment, observed her healthy appetite, the precise but intensely feminine movements of her hands, the manner in which she sampled each mouthful.

Poetry in motion. There was no guile, no studied orchestration. He wondered what she would look like with her hair loose, and spread over his pillow as she slept. Or tossed and dishevelled in the throes of passion as she rode him hard and fast.

She possessed a beautiful mouth, even white teeth. Was she well versed in using both to drive a man wild and hold him on the knife-edge between pleasure and pain?

Confrontational, no artifice, he mused thoughtfully. What you saw was what you got.

Yet she wasn't above playing a diverse game. For the sheer hell of it, he suspected, as he mentally reviewed the exotic meals she'd delivered all three evenings. He'd expected unimaginative fare. Not the dishes she'd gone to a great deal of trouble to prepare.

His eyes acquired a gleam of dancing amusement. What did she have in mind for tonight?

Anneke sensed his gaze, caught the musing glint apparent, and spared him a level look. 'Nice to know I amuse you. Perhaps you could be specific?'

Sebastian banked down the laughter, broke off a piece of bread and ate it, then offered her a warm smile. 'How specific would you like me to be?'

She watched the powerful movement of his jaw, the

way his facial muscles clenched and relaxed, the smooth column of his throat. His hands fascinated her. Broad palms, strong wrists, tanned skin stretched over fluid sinew, long, tapered fingers that belied their strength, clean, well-shaped nails.

'Oh, the whole truth and nothing but the truth will do.'

'I'm curious to know where you learnt to cook.'

She effected a light shrug. 'A young chef rented the apartment next to mine for a while. I helped him perfect his English, and in return he shared his culinary skills.'

'Among other skills?'

She didn't pretend to misunderstand his meaning. 'He wasn't my lover.' She replaced her cutlery, then carefully pushed her plate aside and stood to her feet. 'Thanks for lunch.'

He'd offended her. Interesting. 'Sit down.'

'No.' Her eyes flared, darkening to the deepest emerald flecked with gold. Without a word she turned and walked from the room, out onto the pavement and into the sunshine.

She lifted a hand and slid her sunglasses down from atop her head, and walked along the street towards her car.

'You left these behind.'

Anneke heard Sebastian's faintly accented drawl, paused, then turned and threw him a fulminating glare.

He had her carry-bags secured in each hand, but made no effort to pass them to her.

'I'll take them.' She reached out, only to scream in silent frustration as he fell into step beside her. 'Don't,' she warned in a deadly quiet voice, 'think you're safe, just because we're in a public place.'

He looked at her with studied ease, aware from the set

of her shoulders, the slightly clenched fists, that she meant what she said.

'We're almost at the car park.'

'You don't need to play the gentleman,' she retaliated with heavy sarcasm.

'In this instance, I choose to.' He scanned the wide apron of bitumen with its lines of parked cars, identified hers, and crossed towards it.

Anneke walked ahead of him and unlocked and opened the passenger door, then stood aside as he placed the carry-bags onto the seat.

He straightened, and she was suddenly intensely aware of his height, his proximity, and the faint musky aroma of cologne and man.

He looked down at her, saw the tilt of her chin, the residue of anger that tightened her expression. Without a word he lifted a hand and trailed the tips of his fingers down one cheek and splayed them along her jaw.

Then he smiled and lowered his head down to hers, capturing her mouth with his own in a gentle evocative kiss that was all too brief.

'Drive carefully.' Without a further word he turned and navigated a line of cars to his own powerful Range Rover.

Frustrating, *irritating* man, she accorded, adding a few descriptive and vividly pithy curses as she crossed round and slid in behind the wheel.

She reversed, then eased her sedan out onto the street. By the time she arrived at her aunt's cottage she had devised numerous ways to render him grievous bodily harm, as well as concocting the most bizarre series of menus that she could summon to mind.

Anneke unpacked the carry-bags, poured herself a cold

drink, and checked her watch. Three hours until she needed to begin dinner preparations.

Housework, she decided. She'd clean and dust and polish. Busy hands, healthy mind. Well, hers was filled with vengeful thoughts, which somehow made a mockery of that particular saying.

When she'd finished, everything sparkled and the cottage was redolent with the smell of beeswax. And the richness of freshly baked fruit cake.

It was after five when her mobile rang, and without thinking she wiped her hands, then reached for the unit and activated it.

Nothing. Only an eerie silence echoed her customary greeting. Her fingers shook slightly as she disengaged the phone.

Rationale dictated it was just a crank call. She doubted it was Adam. Although she couldn't discount the possibility he might take a perverse delight in causing her a degree of nervous anxiety.

It was just after six when she delivered Sebastian's evening meal.

'Stay and have a drink with me.'

Anneke looked at him, saw the unbound hair and noted its unruly state—almost as if he'd raked his fingers through the length on more than one occasion.

Maybe the plot wasn't working out, or the characters weren't performing as they should. Or he was struggling through a bout of writer's block.

'Thanks, but I don't drink.' Not entirely true. She adored good French champagne, and reserved the partaking of it for special occasions. As this wasn't one of them, and she seriously doubted he had a bottle of Dom Perignon or

Cristal on ice, it was simpler to decline. 'Your meal will get cold, and so will mine,' she said easily, and turned towards the door.

He made no attempt to dissuade her, and when the door closed behind her he crossed to the table, removed the cover and examined the contents of the tray.

It could have been worse. He moved to the bank of cupboards, took out a skillet and reached into the refrigerator for a large T-bone steak.

When it came to the dessert, he scraped off the cream, took a tentative bite, then opted for fresh fruit. He washed it down with bottled mineral water, then spooned freshly ground beans into the coffee-maker, poured water into the cylinder and switched it on.

The glass carafe had just begun to fill when there was a crashing sound from the adjoining cottage.

He was out of the door and running, Shaef at his side, adrenalin pumping, his mind actively selecting one scenario after another as he covered the set of steps in one leap and pounded on the door.

CHAPTER FIVE

A MUFFLED and very explicit curse fell from Anneke's lips as she surveyed the mess at her feet.

Cut flowers were strewn in an arc across the floor, water pooled in a widening puddle, and Aunt Vivienne's prized Waterford crystal vase lay shattered in a hundred shards on the laundry's ceramic-tiled floor.

There was no one to blame but herself. Unless she counted a fractional second's distraction at the insistent and distinctive peal of her mobile telephone.

'Anneke.' Forceful, authoritative, *demanding*. Sebastian's voice penetrated the evening's stillness, accompanied by the heavy, insistent rap of knuckles on wood.

'OK, OK,' she responded in resigned exasperation. 'I'm in the…' Her voice trailed to a halt as he appeared at the screened laundry door.

'Hell,' he cursed quietly, taking in the scene at a glance. Her legs were bare, so were her feet.

'Apt,' she responded drily.

'Don't move. I'll be back.'

He was, within minutes, with a bucket, pan and brush.

'Don't throw out the flowers.'

'They're likely to contain hidden pieces of glass.'

'Crystal,' she corrected without thought, and incurred a dark, sweeping glance.

'Waterford, thirty-five years old, wedding gift. You want the pattern detail?'

'There's no need to be facetious.'

'Likewise, you don't need to be so particular.'

'Oh, go soak your head in a bucket!'

His smile held a certain grimness. 'Nice to have your gratitude.'

She wanted to burst into tears. She treasured beautiful things. Loved the art and symmetry of exquisite crystal and porcelain. To have a piece break by her own hand was almost akin to killing a living thing.

He glimpsed the momentary desolation, caught a flash of something deeper, and fought the temptation to pull her into his arms. Such an action, he knew, would only earn him the sharp edge of her tongue.

'Vivienne has plenty more flowers in the garden,' he offered mildly, ignoring her protest as he deftly swept everything into the bucket, then dealt with the water.

'Vacuum cleaner. Hall cupboard?' Had to be. Both cottages were similar in design.

Twice the vacuum hose rattled as the cleaner sucked up undetected shards of crystal, and she stepped onto a towel he spread on the floor while he completed the task.

'Thanks,' she added, aware she owed him that, at least. She could have coped, dispensing with the mess, but it was likely she'd have cut herself in the process.

Dammit, she didn't want to owe him. Nor did she particularly covet his company. He made her feel…uncomfortable, she conceded reluctantly.

As if he was all too aware of the sexual chemistry

between them, and content to wait and watch for the moment *she* felt it.

Well, she had news for him. She could pin it down to the precise moment she'd walked into Aunt Vivienne's kitchen the first night she arrived and found him there making tea. For her.

Sebastian watched the fleeting emotions chase across her expressive features, divined the reason for them, and kept his own expression deliberately bland.

She could tell him to go, or ask him to stay. There was always tomorrow, the day after that. And he was a patient man.

The tussle between politeness and impoliteness warred, and there was really no contest. 'Would you like some coffee?'

He studied her in silence for a few seconds. 'Thanks.'

In the kitchen she set the coffee-maker up, then extracted two cups and saucers, added a bowl of sugar, and took cream from the refrigerator.

Anneke was conscious of him as he leant one hip against the servery. His tall frame made the kitchen seem smaller, and she became aware of every move she made. Only sheer habit prevented the spoon clattering onto the saucer, and she was extremely careful with the glass carafe as she poured hot coffee.

Sebastian collected both cups and set them down on the dining room table, then he pulled out a chair and folded his length into it.

She crossed to the table and sat opposite him. Conversational skills were something she'd rarely lacked. Yet at this precise moment she had trouble summoning one topic to mind.

'How's the book going?'

An amused gleam momentarily lit his eyes before he successfully hid it by letting his eyelids droop fractionally. The inevitable question an author had to field from time to time. 'My answer would only seem a paradox.'

The dry response made it easy for her to resort to humour. 'You've hit a bad patch?'

He winced mentally. 'You could say I've dug myself into a hole and I can't see a way out.'

'Why not back up and avoid the hole altogether?'

Good point. 'I need to think about it a while.'

'So sharing coffee and conversation is really an excuse not to stare at a blank screen and curse beneath your breath?'

'Perhaps I couldn't resist your charming company.'

Icily polite. Furiously angry. Indignant, voluble, even sarcastic. At no stage could she recall being charming. Maybe it was time to try.

'Tell me why you write.'

'Curiosity, or genuine interest?'

'A bit of both,' she answered honestly.

'An obsessive need to create a story.' A statement which usually brought a non-committal response, indicating un-interest or lack of comprehension.

Anneke looked at him carefully. Glimpsed the fine lines fanning out from the corners of his eyes, the faint furrow creasing his forehead, as if he'd frowned in concentration too often in the past few hours.

'And the *how* of it?'

His mouth quirked. 'Matching the image in my head with words that allow the reader to capture my vision.'

An art form that wasn't always easy, requiring dedica-

tion and discipline, she perceived. There could be no doubt
Sebastian Lanier possessed both qualities.

He waited for the inevitable comments relating to fame
and fortune, the media circus he went to great pains to
avoid. But none were forthcoming.

Inane questions weren't her practice. 'It must be a fascinating process.' Her eyes glinted with humour. 'And not
without a degree of frustration when the words don't flow
as you need them to.'

His smile held a warmth that made her stomach curl.
And the eyes were dark, gleaming and steady. Assessing,
analytical, almost as if he had calculated every move, every
angle, and was waiting to see which one she would choose.

It gave her an uncanny feeling.

'Mind if I pour more coffee?'

His voice was husky and held a tinge of humour, almost
as if he'd read her mind.

'Of course not. Help yourself.'

He indicated her cup. 'Want me to refill yours?'

It was strong, really strong. If she drank another, she'd
be awake half the night. 'No, thanks. I'll have water instead.'

He crossed to the servery, helped himself from the
coffee-maker, then reached into a nearby cupboard, extracted a glass and filled it with water. All with the ease of
a man who was familiar with her aunt's kitchen.

She could almost imagine their easy friendship, and experienced a pang of envy.

He should get out of here. The computer beckoned, and
he'd just had a fleeting but inspired flash as to how he could
circumvent the current plot hole.

However, the coffee was good, really good. And
Anneke's current mood intrigued him.

He placed the glass down onto the table in front of her, then slid into his chair.

'Your turn.'

Her eyes widened, the light, clear green darkening fractionally as comprehension hit.

Fascinating…eyes a man could drown in, and he discovered he wanted to, very much. Thread a hand through her silky hair and hold fast her head while he shaped her mouth with his own. Anchor her against him so she felt his need while he heightened her own. The slow erotic glide of hands, lips, until neither was enough and the barrier of clothes proved too much.

'You live in Sydney, and work in a legal office,' Sebastian prompted, banking down libidinous images.

'No longer work in one specific legal office,' Anneke corrected drily.

'Resigned?'

'Walked out.'

His eyes held a humorous gleam. 'Problems with the boss?'

She looked at him in measured silence. 'You could say that.' A statement she didn't intend to clarify.

At that moment the phone rang, its double peal insistent, and her eyes flared momentarily with apprehension.

Another nuisance call?

Sebastian unbent his lengthy frame and pushed in his chair. 'I'll let you get that.' He drained the remains of his coffee and carried the cup and saucer to the servery. Then he lifted a hand in silent salute and let himself out of the back door.

Anneke crossed to the phone, removed the receiver, and

experienced relief when she discovered the caller was one of her aunt's friends.

A relief which proved short-lived when the phone rang again minutes later.

She tossed up whether to answer it or not, for she couldn't discount the possibility it might be a legitimate call. Indecision warred for a few seconds, then she took a deep breath and unhooked the receiver.

Her heart sank. No answer, only heavy breathing. She resisted the temptation to crash the receiver down on its cradle. 'Damn you,' she said fiercely. 'Try this again, and I'll contact the police and have them put a trace on the line.'

There was the faint click of a receiver being replaced, then the hollow sound of a cut connection.

'Problems?'

Anneke whirled at the sound of that deep, faintly accented voice, and saw Sebastian, tray in hand, standing just inside the kitchen door.

Her heart was thumping in her chest, and her eyes, she knew, were stark and wide. Control kicked in, and she forced her voice into even tones.

'You heard.' There was no point in pretending he hadn't.

With ease, he crossed the room and deposited the tray on the servery. 'You didn't answer the question.'

Why fabricate? 'Someone seems to be having fun at my expense.'

He leant a hip against the cabinet and regarded her carefully, noting a face devoid of colour, eyes that were far too dark. 'How many such calls have you taken?'

'That was the sixth call in three days, if you count my mobile.'

'He's persistent.' He waited a beat. 'Abusive?'

Anneke shook her head. 'So far he hasn't said a word.'

'Tomorrow we notify the phone company and arrange an unlisted number.' His eyes hardened, and he kept them partially hooded. 'Shaef stays with you.'

'*We?* I can take care of it. And I don't need Shaef.'

'It's Shaef or me. Choose.'

She shot him a look of disbelief. 'Aren't you going just a tiny bit overboard with this?'

His eyes were obsidian, his gaze hard and unblinking. 'No.'

Anneke drew in a deep breath, considered telling Sebastian to go take a running hike, then thought better of it.

'It's probably a random call by some idle teenager who, hearing a female voice on the line, has decided to play a stupid game.'

'Maybe.'

'You think it's my ex-boss? If he's caught, and I press charges, the Law Society will suspend him from practice,' she qualified slowly. 'Why take the risk?'

Sebastian's gaze remained steady. 'Some men get their kicks skating close to the edge.'

'He already has my mobile number. Why not use that instead of the house phone?'

'It's too simple. He wants you to be aware he knows where you are.'

Her eyes darkened until they resembled the deepest emerald. Was Adam that cunning? That devious? She could recall telling him she had an aunt who lived in a cottage on a northern coastal beach, but she was willing to swear she hadn't mentioned Aunt Vivienne's surname, or *which* north-coast beach.

Get a grip, she mentally cautioned. You're not in any danger.

'Don't answer the house phone, and switch your mobile onto voice mail.'

'Any more instructions?'

'Don't be sassy.'

He loomed too close for comfort, and it took an effort not to step back a pace. 'You've done your good deed for the day. Twice over.'

'Is that a subtle hint for me to leave?'

'I'd hate to keep you from your work.'

'The computer can wait,' Sebastian drawled, moving forward a pace. 'This won't.'

'This' was his mouth on hers in what proved to be a devastating invasion. He possessed the touch, the instinctive mastery to make a kiss seem like an extension of the physical act itself.

Worse, to make a woman feel a kiss was nowhere near *enough*. That there was more, much more to savour in the realm of sensual delight.

A demanding lover, Sebastian Lanier would take everything a woman offered, and encourage her to give more.

Anneke suppressed a slight shiver. The reward would be magnificent, she acquiesced. Electrifying.

Her heart pounded, and her pulse raced almost out of control as he trailed his mouth to the edge of her jaw. She cried out as he savoured the column of her throat, and she arched her head to allow him greater access.

His hands were warm against her clothing as they moulded her close, and the barrier was something to be dispensed with as the need arose for skin against skin.

Sebastian was the first to move, tugging her blouse free, his fingers deft with buttons as he freed each and every one.

Her own sought purchase on soft cotton, and yanked hard until the tee-shirt slipped out from his waistband.

Dear Lord, he felt good. Hard ribs, corded muscles, broad back, wide shoulders. Her hands curved higher, then clung as he crushed her to him.

His mouth claimed, *staked* a possession that brooked no denial, and for one brief second she almost threw common sense out of the window.

Sebastian was aware the exact moment she began to retreat, and he reluctantly and very slowly broke the kiss, allowing his lips to brush hers, savouring each corner, then he pushed her gently to arm's length.

'I want to take you to bed.' A faint smile curved his lips. 'But I have the feeling you'd only hate me in the morning.'

As well as herself. Twisted sheets and an energetic coupling wasn't on her agenda. With any man.

'I'll write down my phone number. Should anything go bump in the night, call me.' He slid a hand to her cheek, cupped it, and traced her lips with his thumb. 'OK?'

Anneke inclined her head fractionally.

'I'll whistle up Shaef.'

Five minutes later the Alsatian was instructed who he had to guard, and how. Both doors were securely locked, and Anneke settled herself in bed with a good book.

It was after eleven when she put out the light, and on the edge of sleep it was Sebastian's image which came to mind. His sculpted features, the piercing grey eyes that saw too much.

Someone who had experienced more than his share, and had dealt with it. Only a fool would surmise otherwise.

She thought of his kiss, the way his mouth felt on her own, the familiarity of his hands as they moulded her body. And hated herself for wanting more.

CHAPTER SIX

ANNEKE woke early, stretched, then slid out of bed and almost stepped onto a sleek-coated animal curled protectively on the floor. A very large animal.

Oh, my God. *Shaef.*

Memory surfaced in one fell swoop, and a soft curse fell from her lips.

With considerable caution she skirted round the dog and crossed to the bathroom. The dog followed.

Five minutes later she returned to the bedroom, filching her swimsuit from the shower stall where she'd hung it over the taps to dry.

It fitted snug over her slender curves, and she pulled on sweat-shorts and top, then made her way into the kitchen.

Fresh orange juice added a certain zing to her palate, and she looked at the dog with a degree of doubt.

'OK, I guess you need to go outside. Water,' she declared decisively, and hunted for a bowl. 'Food.' The dog's ears pricked at the mention of it.

Dammit, she was a cat person. Dogs gnawed on bones, ate meat, and munched on dry food. A goodly amount of each, she surmised, judging by Shaef's size. None of which she had on hand.

'Sorry, fella.' She placed a bowl filled with water onto the floor. 'This will have to do for now, then you can go home for breakfast.'

When she let him out of the back door, he promptly lolloped to the nearest tree, then, considerably more comfortable, returned to sit on the step.

'Divided loyalties, pal. I'm going for a run along the beach. You get to choose whether you guard me or the house.' She smiled and leant down to fondle one silky ear. 'Personally, I'd go for the house.'

He didn't, of course. She hadn't moved more than half a dozen steps when he fell in beside her. 'Well, there's no doubt you take after your owner,' she said conversationally. 'He's every bit as stubborn as you are.'

Anneke reached the beach and sprinted down onto the sand. And saw Sebastian engaged in callisthenics. Waiting to join her?

Sebastian *plus* his dog? She sprinted towards him. 'Been waiting long?' she queried sweetly.

He wasn't deceived by the mildness of her tone. She was angry. Well, he could handle it. He drew himself up to his full height with ease, placed a hand on one hip and offered her a warm smile.

'Beautiful day.'

She'd slept well. It made the fact that he hadn't seem worthwhile.

'Should I put this down to chance? Or is your appearance on the beach at this hour a forerunner of things to come?'

My, she possessed a sharp tongue. He had an urge to take her mouth with his own and change tart to something smooth and sweet.

'You object to my company?'

She placed a hand on each hip, taking defiance to a new level. 'In the thinly veiled guise of bodyguard, *yes*.'

He had to work hard to prevent humour from entering his voice. 'Are you saying only one of us gets to share your run?'

Damn him, he was amused. 'Given a choice, Shaef wins out.' Her eyes searched his, saw the purposeful intent evident, and she released a deep sigh. 'But you're not going to give me a choice, are you?'

'No.'

'I just might have to hit you.'

'Think carefully before you do.'

There was a silkiness evident in his tone that sent a faint shiver down the length of her spine.

Without a further word she turned and broke into a run, aware of the moment he joined her, man and dog matching their stride to hers. Part of her wanted to set a punishing pace, but she knew she'd never outrun either of them.

A degree of resentment rose to the surface. Against Adam, if it was he who'd initiated a nuisance campaign, but primarily with Sebastian, for any number of reasons, she decided darkly. Foremost, for tugging at her emotions and turning them every which way but loose.

The sandy cove curved out to sea in a low outcrop of rocks, and Anneke turned when she reached that point and began retracing her steps without pause.

Shaef was having a wonderful time, bounding on ahead, then diverging down to the incoming tide to examine a shell or a piece of seaweed. Sebastian jogged steadily at her side.

It was a relief to draw level with her towel, and without saying so much as a word she pulled off her joggers, stripped down to her swimsuit, and sprinted lightly down to the water's edge.

She fully expected Sebastian to join her, and silently vowed as she dived into the cool sea that he'd regret it if he did. Quite *how* she'd ensure he regretted it, she wasn't clear.

Sebastian intuitively opted to engage Shaef in a game of throw-the-stick until Anneke emerged.

'Wise,' she muttered beneath her breath, and missed the amused gleam in his dark eyes as he called Shaef to heel.

'Share breakfast with me.'

She was sharing his dog, his protection. That was enough. She caught up the towel and wound it sarong-wise round her waist. 'Thanks, but no, thanks. I have a heap of things to do.'

He snared her wrist as she turned to walk away from him. 'Lock the cottage securely if you go anywhere. Drive with the central locking system in place. And make sure you park the car on a main thoroughfare.'

She began to steam with indignation. 'Anything else?'

'Carry your mobile phone at all times.'

'I'm amazed you haven't mentioned Shaef.'

'That's a given,' Sebastian intoned hardily. 'Where you go, he goes.'

The steam changed to smoke. 'Now just a tiny minute, here.' Anneke lifted a hand and poked his chest. Hard. 'If my heavy breather is Adam, he's hundreds of miles south in Sydney. A nuisance, but not a threat.'

'And if it's not Adam?'

Ice chilled her veins. 'I intend to find out one way or another. Meantime, stay off my back.' She poked his chest again for good measure, then tugged her hand free and marched back to the cottage.

Impossible, dictatorial, *stubborn* man. Who did he think he was? And by what right did he imagine he could tell her what to do?

Sebastian watched her retreating form, and that of Shaef, who, at a click of Sebastian's fingers, had taken a few bounding strides to fall in at Anneke's side.

A woman who would give as good as she got, and be passionate in giving it… Be it anger, or making love. The former he could handle with one hand tied behind his back. It was the latter that bothered him.

He could have done with cooling down in the ocean himself, and he measured the time it would take her to shower, make coffee, eat whatever it was she had for breakfast, then begin making phone calls.

At the very least he had ten minutes, even if she messed up the order of things.

Anneke entered the cottage and headed straight for the shower, where she sluiced off the salt water and shampooed her hair. Then, towelled dry, she dressed in sapphire-blue shorts and a matching sleeveless top.

Coffee, hot, sweet, strong and black, then she'd fill a bowl with cereal and fruit.

It was after eight when she crossed to the phone. Aunt Vivienne was first on her list, and, after eliciting news that Elise was fine, she gave her aunt relevant details and relayed the fact that until she contacted the police she had no idea whether they'd put a trace on the line or suggest she apply for an unlisted number. Either way, Aunt Vivienne's permission was essential.

Next came a call to the phone company, who, on receiving relevant details, promised to check their records and ring back.

Which left the police. Two 'on hold's and two transfers later, she connected with a very informative young man.

'Yes, ma'am. The complaint was logged in at twentyo-five hundred hours last night by a Sebastian Lanier acting on behalf of Vivienne Sorrel, owner of the property. The duty officer advised appropriate action, which I understand is being taken, pending authority this morning from Vivienne Sorrel. Perhaps you might like to check with Sebastian Lanier?'

Check with him? She'd kill him! 'Thank you.' She replaced the receiver with care, then turned and marched from the cottage, closing the distance between both residences in swift, angry strides.

The back door was open, the screen door unlatched, and she knocked once, then entered to find Sebastian crisping bacon in the microwave while eggs simmered in a pan atop the stove.

'What God-given right do you think you have to log in a report with the police on my behalf?' Anneke demanded wrathfully.

The toaster popped up crisped bread, and he crossed to the servery, removed both slices and calmly buttered them.

'You're angry.'

Emerald fire flashed in her eyes, and she had to clench her fists to refrain from lashing out at him. 'You bet your sweet life I am.'

He glanced up, and shot her a direct look as he extracted a plate from the cupboard. 'I thought it wise to instigate immediate enquiries.'

'Just *who* in hell do you think you are?'

He placed the toast onto the plate. 'I promised Vivienne I'd keep an eye on you.'

'Well, you can take your damned eye off me, as of now.'

Sebastian deftly removed the pan, slid eggs onto toast, collected the bacon, and carried both plates to the table.

'Want to share?'

'No, I don't want to share *anything* with you!' She drew in a deep breath and released it. 'Nothing, *nada*, *niente*. Do you understand?'

He filled a mug with steaming aromatic black coffee, stirred in sugar, and savoured a mouthful. His shoulders lifted in a deliberate Gallic shrug. 'That's certainly specific.'

Anneke flung her arms in the air in a gesture of enraged despair. 'You're not going to do as I ask, are you?'

His eyes pierced hers, dark, dangerous and lethal. 'No.' He picked up cutlery and cut a neat slice from the corner of his toast. 'Not until the nuisance calls stop.'

'I'm twenty-seven years old, not seventeen. I've lived alone for seven years in a city known for its high crime rate. I can take care of myself.'

Sebastian forked a mouthful of toast and egg into his mouth, chewed and swallowed it, then proceeded to cut another slice.

'You've forgotten one thing.'

The anger was still evident, simmering beneath the surface. 'And what, pray, is that?'

'I gave Vivienne my word.'

'And your word is sacrosanct,' Anneke declared with marked cynicism.

'Yes.'

'So get used to it?'

'I'm simply telling you how it is,' he said calmly.

'In that case, there's nothing more to say.'

'No.'

There were *several* more words she could have uttered, many of them blistering and not in the least ladylike. However, restraint in this instance was a favoured option.

'Fine.' She turned towards the back door and walked from his kitchen, then crossed the stretch of lawn and garden separating each cottage.

Her car stood in the carport, and, making a split-second decision, she went indoors, changed her clothes, caught up her bag and mobile phone, then locked up the cottage, slid behind the wheel and reversed down the driveway.

Within minutes she gained the main road leading onto the northern highway. The Gold Coast was only two hours' drive away. Shopping centres, movies, glitzy boutiques. Just the place to escape to, Anneke decided.

She had travelled less than five minutes when her mobile phone rang, and she automatically activated it.

'Tell me where you're going, and what time you expect to be home.'

Her stomach performed a backwards somersault at the sound of Sebastian's voice on the line. It sounded impossibly deep, his accent more pronounced.

Anneke took a deep, steadying breath. 'Go to hell.' Then she cut the connection.

It should have made her feel better. Instead, she felt more and more like an angry juvenile kicking out against authority.

Examining the situation analytically, she was allowing emotions to overrule common sense.

Damn. She thumped a fist against the steering wheel. This contrary ambivalence was ridiculous.

Without further thought she slowed down and pulled off to the side of the road. She caught up her mobile phone and prepared to punch in digits she realised she didn't have. Sure, he'd written down his number, but that was on a piece of paper tucked into a teletex in her aunt's kitchen.

OK, all she had to do was ring directory service. Two minutes later she de-activated the call, and groaned with frustration. Sebastian Lanier's phone number was ex-directory.

One car passed, then another. She didn't notice the Range Rover ease to a halt behind her, nor was she aware as the driver slid out from behind the wheel and trod the bitumen to the passenger side of her car.

A firm tap on the glass was the first indication she had of anyone's presence.

Anneke's head swung towards the window, and even as her elbow moved in automatic reflex to punch down the central locking device the passenger door opened and Sebastian slid into the passenger seat.

His eyes were dark, almost black, his expression grim and unrelenting.

'Careless,' he drawled. 'Very careless.'

'My knight in shining armour,' Anneke mocked. Her eyes were sheer crystalline emerald.

One day soon he would take that spitting tongue of hers and tame it. Was she aware just how close he was to doing it now?

His eyes seared hers as he placed an arm along the top of her seat. 'Co-operate, Anneke, and we'll get along fine.'

It was impossible to ignore the clean male smell of him, the faint aroma of aftershave. Just as it was impossible to dismiss the way her pulse tripped and raced to a quickened beat in his presence.

'The moment the police discover the source of your nuisance calls,' Sebastian assured her with a degree of cynicism, 'you're as free as a bird.' His expression hardened. 'Now, tell me where you're going, what time you expect to return.'

Her chin tilted and her eyes assumed a fiery brilliance. 'What if I don't?'

'That was the first option,' Sebastian said hardily. 'The second is for me to tag along with you.'

'Don't be ridiculous!'

'Choose, Anneke.'

'And if I don't have any set plans?'

'The second option applies.'

Why was she fighting him? She couldn't win. He wouldn't allow it.

She took a deep breath, then slowly released it and handed him her mobile phone. 'Press "redial", and you'll discover I was trying to reach you for the sole purpose of relaying my whereabouts on the Gold Coast and estimated time of return.' When he didn't take the phone, she hit the 'redial' button and pressed the unit to his ear. 'Except your number is ex-directory, and not even the citing of an emergency would reveal it.'

She delved into her bag, pulled out a piece of paper and a pen and thrust them at him, watching as he stroked a series of digits, then handed back the paper.

'Satisfied?' she demanded.

'Ring me when you leave the Coast.'

It wasn't negotiable, and she didn't even bother to refuse him. Although it was impossible not to resort to sarcasm. 'Do we synchronise our watches?'

Sebastian cast her a look that was more expressive than mere words, then he reached for the door clasp and slid out from the seat. 'Drive carefully.'

He closed the door, then covered the distance to his Range Rover.

Anneke watched him in the rear vision mirror, then she activated the ignition, eased the car onto the road.

It should have been a wonderful day. The sun shone brightly in a clear azure sky. The temperature soared to a midsummer high. With only two weeks to go before Christmas, the shops bore colourful decorations and there was an air of expectancy among the many shoppers filling the malls and walkways.

Christmas carols, and a store Santa handing out lollies and balloons to eager children added festive anticipatory cheer.

Anneke had thought to spend Christmas with Aunt Vivienne, but now it appeared she'd be spending it alone.

She could fly to Seattle, join her mother and stepfather for a 'yours, mine and ours' family Christmas.

Or, alternatively, there was her father, happily ensconced in London, who would welcome her into *his* extended family.

A small body careened into her legs, and she held onto the runaway child, soothing the little boy until a harassed and very pregnant young mother caught up to him.

Within minutes her mobile phone rang, and after a moment's hesitation she answered the call. There was a sense of relief to discover it was a friend from Sydney, wanting to exchange mutual news. Difficult in the face of that friendship not to reveal her whereabouts, although 'the Gold Coast' was hardly a fabrication. She simply didn't add that she was only there for the day.

Lunch comprised a salad sandwich washed down by mineral water in an upmarket café, and afterwards she selected a number of Christmas cards.

Her mobile phone rang again while she hovered in a specialist boutique specialising in imported toiletries, and she gave the sales assistant a helpless shrug accompanied by a faint smile, then moved to one side to gain a little privacy.

'Anneke.' The familiar male voice was quiet, almost restrained, but very clear on the line, and her stomach flipped as she gripped the phone.

'Adam.' Calm, keep calm. Act nonchalant, a tiny voice persisted.

'Bitch,' he hissed before she had a chance to disconnect the call. 'No woman runs out on me.'

'There's a first time for everything,' she said crisply. 'Chalk it up to experience.'

'Didn't think I could find you, did you, sweetheart?'

Relief, revulsion…both washed over her in realisation that Adam had been the source. 'Making nuisance calls wasn't very smart, Adam.'

'Payback time,' he dismissed. His voice lowered to a seductive drawl. 'You should have played with me; we could have had a ball.' He proceeded to explain his sexual preferences in graphic detail. 'Pity, but I value my skin, and you've proven to be way too much trouble. *Ciao*, darling. Have a good life.'

Anneke closed the phone and replaced it in her bag. She should, she silently castigated herself, have cut the connection as soon as she heard his voice. Now she simply felt angry, sickened, as his words echoed and reechoed inside her head.

CHAPTER SEVEN

THE impetus to continue shopping was sadly lacking. She needed a different image, something to distract her from dwelling on Adam's bitter invective.

There was a multiple number of cinemas within the shopping complex. She'd go buy a ticket and choose a film to view.

A film about the *Titanic* was currently showing, and it was after six when she entered the car park, located her car and slid in behind the wheel.

Her mobile phone message-bank listed that two calls had been received during her cinema sojourn. One was from Sebastian, the other from the police. She contacted the duty sergeant at the designated number, who relayed the fact that trace on her aunt's telephone had been successful, then contacted Sebastian.

He picked up on the second ring. 'Lanier.'

A concise, deep voice that had the ability to raise goose-bumps on the surface of her skin.

'Anneke.' She barely paused a second. 'I'm leaving now.' She cut the connection, then switched on the ignition and eased the car down several floors to street level.

The drive to Byron Bay was uneventful, and soon after

crossing the Queensland-New South Wales border she passed paddocks high with mature sugar cane. Banana plantations dotted the distant rolling hills, and there were avocado farms, and rich, fertile soil revealing row upon row of pineapples.

Dusk fell swiftly, the shadows lengthening and deepening as light gave way to dark, and it was almost nine when she pulled in beneath the carport adjacent her aunt's cottage.

She switched off the ignition, left her numerous purchases in the boot, then locked the car and trod the path to Sebastian's back door.

Five minutes, ten at the most, then she'd leave.

The screen door was unlocked, and Shaef stood on the other side, tail swishing back and forth in welcome.

Anneke knocked and entered the kitchen, then moved down the hall. Sebastian had had part of the wall between two bedrooms removed. A large executive desk complete with a state-of-the-art computer sat in the middle of one room, and the other was lined from floor to ceiling with bookshelves. In the centre of the room was a large antique buttoned leather armchair, with a matching ottoman, and a standard lamp. Combined, it made a large office-cum-library.

He looked up from the sheaf of papers he was studying, and leaned back in his chair.

'Take a seat.' He indicated one of two sited on the other side of the desk.

'I'd really prefer to keep this short.'

He noted the weary curve of her shoulders, the faint lines of strain marring an otherwise smooth forehead.

Shaef moved forward, nuzzled her hand, then slumped at her feet.

Sebastian sent her a long, considering look. 'Sit down.'

'Still giving orders?'

He ignored the sally, his eyes dark and far too discerning. 'Have you eaten?'

Food, in any shape or form, would probably make her ill. 'I had something earlier.' It wasn't exactly a lie.

'I'll make some tea.' He rose to his feet, crossed round the desk, then moved into the hall.

Anneke could hear the distant sound of water flowing from a tap, the faint hum of an electric kettle as it heated, the chink of crockery.

She closed her eyes. It had been a hell of a day. And it wasn't over yet.

Sebastian re-entered the room, saw the fringe of lashes touching each cheek, the pale, translucent skin.

She was beat, and without doubt emotionally exhausted.

He placed the cup and saucer near the edge of the desk, and watched her nostrils flare slightly as the aroma of bergamot teased the air. Her lashes lifted, then swept upwards in a slow, curving arc.

'Thanks.'

It was hot, heaven, and sweeter than she preferred. She took another appreciative sip, then put the cup carefully back onto the saucer.

'I guess you know the police scored a positive trace to Adam's mobile phone?'

Sebastian leaned one hip against the edge of the desk. 'Yes.'

She tilted her head and looked at him. 'Thank you for your concern.' He deserved that. 'And your help.'

'As I recall, you weren't too keen to accept either,' Sebastian said drily.

No, she hadn't been. 'You were very controlling.'

One eyebrow rose, and his mouth curved with a tinge of humour. 'I'm surprised you don't add "manipulative".'

'That, too,' Anneke agreed.

'Did it ever occur to you to question *why*?'

With just a few words their conversation had taken a subtle shift, and she wasn't comfortable with the change. 'Maybe we can continue this another time.' She stood to her feet, and immediately wished she hadn't, for it brought her much closer to him than she would have liked. 'Although it really isn't necessary, is it?' She took a backward step, and missed the faint gleam of amusement apparent in those dark eyes.

'You think not? Perhaps I'd better clarify it.' He reached for her shoulders and pulled her forward until she stood anchored between his thighs. Then he slowly lowered his head and brushed his lips against her temple. 'Are you beginning to get the picture?'

One hand slid down her back and cupped her buttocks, while the other slipped up to hold fast her head.

'Sebastian—'

His lips feathered down to the edge of her mouth, lingered there, then teased a trail of light kisses along the full lower curve.

'I don't think this is a—'

'Good idea?' He slid his tongue between her lips and felt rather than heard her breath catch.

'No,' Anneke whispered, as her heart raced to a faster beat, and heat flared through her veins.

His mouth was a soft caress as his hands moulded her close.

A kiss, she told herself. That's all it is. Why, she could even persuade herself that it didn't mean anything. Nothing at all. Men had kissed her before, in friendship, affection, and with a lover's passion.

She lifted her hands and linked them together at his nape, then leant in against him to enjoy the sensation of closeness. And came seriously unstuck when his mouth firmed on her own.

He'd kissed her before, as a questing, seeking experiment, and as a form of angry punishment.

This, *this* was different. Very different. It was both possession and promise. And it made her feel terribly afraid.

He had the touch, the instinctive skill of a man well versed in a woman's needs. His hands, his fingers, knew when to glide, where to caress, to drive her wild.

It was as if every sensitive nerve-end quivered in anticipation, then shrieked at each teasing stroke, every light pinch.

Dear God, she was silk, her skin satin-smooth, and each erogenous zone reacted like fire to his touch. He wanted to free her beautiful body of the restriction of clothes, to explore each indentation, each curve, until she moaned with delight, then begged for release.

That it would be him, only him she saw when he drove himself into her and made her his own. And him, only him, who had the power to take her to the brink, then tip her over the edge. He who held her tight and caught her when she fell.

His fingers sought the clip fastening of her bra and deftly released it, then he slid his hand to cup the fullness of her breast, teased its hardened peak, then trailed his mouth down her throat to the creamy crest. And felt her resistance.

What was she doing? This had gone way beyond mutual exploration, or mutual gratitude.

Anneke could feel the evidence of his arousal, the hard potent shaft beneath the zip of his jeans as it pressed high against his belt. Sensual heat emanated from his skin, and the beat of his heart was hard and deep.

His mouth settled on hers, persuasive, evocative and devastatingly sensual.

It would be easy, so very easy to let him take her wherever he wanted to go. To give in to the magic he promised and just enjoy whatever the night might hold.

Yet, no matter what the enticement, casual sex wasn't her style.

It took considerable effort to retreat, to drag her mouth from his and push herself to arm's length. More to quieten her fast-beating heart and attempt to regain her breath.

'I think,' Anneke enunciated unevenly, 'it would be best if I left. Now,' she added, dropping her hands from his arms.

'Best for whom?'

'Me. You. Us,' she added for good measure. 'I mean, there is no *us*.' This was getting worse with every passing second. 'It's just—'

'Quit while you're ahead,' Sebastian advised gently, watching the fleeting change of expression chase across her features as she struggled for control.

He could pull her close, wreak havoc with that beautiful mouth, and take her here. On the desk, the floor. It didn't matter.

And that was the part that bothered him. He'd always displayed *finesse* with a woman. Wining, dining, flowers, pretty compliments. Sex by mutual consent, albeit that it might be wild or restrained. Rarely had he felt the urge to tear clothes from a female body, abrade her skin with his mouth, his hands, and join himself with her like a plundering conqueror.

He admired women...their strengths, their weaknesses, their passion. He respected their innate femininity. And he had enjoyed them. No serious commitment, no strings attached.

Until now.

Now he was captivated as never before by a smile, the way her mouth curved to tilt at the edges. The sweep of long lashes and the lure of a pair of green eyes which lightened or deepened according to mood.

She was fire and ice, passion and fury. And he wanted her in a way that he'd never wanted a woman before.

'Thanks for—' Her voice wasn't quite steady. 'Being there for me.'

He leaned forward and brushed a finger down the slope of her nose. 'My pleasure.'

'Really?' A faint smile teased the edges of her mouth as she moved back a pace. 'We've been at daggers drawn most of the time.'

It was his turn to smile. There was a dangerous quality evident in the darkness of his eyes, a latent passion which, unleashed, would sweep her way out of her depth. It was there in his expression, the forceful set of his features, the stance that was studiously relaxed. Like the watching eye of a tiger, just waiting to pounce.

Go, a tiny voice taunted. Don't linger.

Without a further word she turned and walked from the room, traversed the hall and let herself out of the back door.

Shaef shadowed her steps as she crossed the path connecting the two properties, and she leant forward to fondle his ears as she unlocked the cottage, then sent him on his way before she stepped inside.

The house was quiet, and she took a long, cool shower, slipped on a robe, then she delved into the refrigerator for a light snack.

Television provided instant visual entertainment, but there was little that captured her attention, even less that held her interest.

It had been a long day, and she took time to examine each and every incident in the hope that reflection would bring peace of mind.

Fat chance. All it did was prove she was too wired to simply fall into bed and covet sleep.

In desperation she selected a book, settled into an armchair, and tried to lose herself in the characters and plot of a favourite author.

Five minutes later she thrust it down. On impulse she went into the bedroom, discarded the robe and slipped into shorts and top.

Within seconds she left the cottage and made her way down onto the beach.

The moon was high in the sky, bathing everything with a pale opalescent glow. Shadows from a clump of palm trees cast long fingers over the sand, and the sea was a mass of silver and dappled pewter that stretched right out to the horizon.

Anneke walked along the damp sand left by an outgoing tide, and breathed in deeply of the clean night air.

There was a whimper, a short bark, then Shaef fell in step at her side.

'Unable to sleep?'

She should have known Sebastian would investigate Shaef's departure. Yesterday, even this morning, she would have resented his presence.

'I figured a walk might help.' It was impossible to detect his expression in the moonlight.

They walked in silence for a few minutes, and she was aware of him in a way she found vaguely frightening.

Somehow she'd known he was trouble from the moment she first caught sight of him.

At first she'd thought it was just chemistry. Sensual sexual magnetism at its most potent. An electric awareness that was both foolish and capricious.

'Want to talk about it?'

Anneke heard Sebastian's words, examined them, and took solace from the shadow of semi-darkness. How could she say that it was *he* who was on her mind, *him* disturbing her thoughts?

'Adam rang me this afternoon.'

Sebastian's voice became a silky drawl. 'Foolish of him.'

'Very,' she replied in succinct agreement.

'I imagine the conversation went from bad to worse?'

'You could say that.' She turned her head and looked out over the silver sea. There didn't seem to be any need to fill the gaps in between, or repeat the vicious personal attack. It was over. That was all that mattered.

By tacit consent they turned and began retracing their steps.

'Have dinner with me tomorrow night.'

Anneke directed him a faintly humorous glance. 'You want me to prepare a meal for two, then sit down at your table?'

'I had a seafood restaurant in mind, overlooking Byron Bay. Silver service, wine steward, waiters,' Sebastian indicated with unruffled ease.

'I get to wear stiletto heels, make-up?' She laughed, a

delightful light sound that held genuine mirth. 'OK. You're on. What time?'

'Six.'

When they reached Aunt Vivienne's cottage he stood aside while she inserted the key into the lock, then he turned and cut a leisurely stride to his own home.

She tried to tell herself she wasn't disappointed he'd made no attempt to touch her.

CHAPTER EIGHT

ANNEKE'S wardrobe of formal and semi-formal wear was reasonably extensive. The only problem being that most of that particular range of her clothes hung in the closet of her Sydney apartment.

In her rush to escape her job, Adam and the city, she'd simply dragged down a suitcase and pulled clothes off hangers, out of drawers, and flung them willy-nilly into the case.

Her proposed sojourn on an isolated beach had lent itself to including casual shorts and tops, jeans. Not elegant after-five wear, or extravagant high-heeled pumps.

It was a clear choice between a classic black dress, or a long floral slip.

The black dress won out, and she tended to her make-up with care, left her hair loose, and was about to catch up her purse when she heard Sebastian's Range Rover pull into the driveway.

Anneke reached the door as Sebastian trod the path, and the breath caught in her throat at the sight of him.

Attired in dark tailored trousers, matching jacket, and white shirt and tie, he was the antithesis of the man she was accustomed to seeing every day.

The image unsettled her. It was crazy to feel nervous, but she couldn't prevent the heavy thud of her heart, or the unwarranted apprehension which curled round her nerve-ends.

'Hi,' she greeted brightly. Too brightly?

Polite conversation had never been more difficult, and she waited until Sebastian reached the highway before querying, 'How long have you lived next door to my aunt?'

'Five years.'

'Yet during each of my visits I've never caught sight of you.'

He turned his head and cast her a quick glance. 'I travel around a bit in between finishing one book and starting the next.'

'Publicity tours?'

'Yes. And research.'

'You'd represent a publishing promoter's dream. The height, the arresting looks, combined with more than a hint of the dark and dangerous. The women would flock to the literary luncheons, the book-signings.'

'A compliment, Anneke?' he queried with deceptive mildness. 'Or a condemnation?'

She subjected him to a detailed appraisal, and took her time giving a considered opinion. 'Oh, a compliment.' Her eyes travelled up and met his briefly. 'I don't doubt you handle it all with consummate charm.' Except there would be an absence of ego, she determined silently.

She watched as he entered town and eased the vehicle into a car park. He cut the engine and removed the key from the ignition. 'Shall we go?'

The restaurant Sebastian had chosen specialised in seafood, and she ordered prawn cocktail as a starter, sea perch as a main course with vegetables, and she declined dessert.

Sebastian merely doubled her order, added prawns and scallops to his dish, then requested the wine steward bring champagne.

'We're celebrating?'

He dismissed the tasting ritual, and indicated both flutes be filled. Then he touched the rim of his flute to her own. 'To friendship.'

Friendship? Could a woman be *friend* to a man such as Sebastian Lanier? Somehow Anneke doubted there would be any half-measures. Sebastian might observe the courtship dance, with its seeking manoeuvres, but when he'd staked his claim it would be all or nothing.

She had the strangest feeling that dinner this evening in semi-formal surroundings was the first step he intended she take to...*what*? His bed?

Their starter arrived, and she bit into the first of three succulent prawns doused with a delicate sauce and set on a bed of shredded lettuce.

It was difficult to sit opposite a man at a dinner table and not subconsciously observe the way he ate. Whether he stabbed his food with the fork, how he employed the knife. If his use of the cutlery was precise, or merely utilitarian. Body language, despite an adherence to good manners, tended to be revealing.

'Where will you spend Christmas?'

Anneke lifted her head and was unable to discern much from his gaze. 'I haven't made any definite plans.' She lifted her flute and sipped some champagne, then replaced it down onto the table. 'What about you?'

He pushed his entrée plate to one side and leaned back in his chair. 'Paris.'

The city of love. The Arc de Triomphe, Champs Elysées,

the Eiffel Tower, the Left Bank and the River Seine. Misty grey skies, drizzling rain, the cold. But the ambience...

Anneke stifled a sigh. 'You have family there?'

'Grandmère.' His expression softened, his mouth relaxed and his eyes held reflective warmth. 'Her eightieth birthday falls on Christmas Day.'

She could imagine the gathering, and felt vaguely envious. To be involved, to be part of it... The laughter, love. Gifts and giving.

'When do you fly out?'

'Friday week.'

A lump settled inside her stomach. In eight days he would leave, and when he returned she'd be gone.

The waiter appeared with their main course, and she viewed the grilled sea perch with its artistically displayed vegetables with perfunctory interest. All of a sudden her appetite seemed to have fled.

How long had she known this man? A week? Yet, while his presence had alternately annoyed and inflamed her, there was a pull of the senses, almost as if something was exigent, forcing recognition on some deep, primal level.

There was a part of her that urged compliance, a devilish spontaneity uncaring of anything except *now*.

And that was dangerous. Infinitely dangerous. Somehow she couldn't imagine it being easy to sample what Sebastian Lanier had to offer, then calmly turn and walk away.

It was better, far better not to engage in anything at all. Besides, what could happen in a week?

Anneke picked at the fish, sampled each of the vegetables, returned to the fish, then replaced her cutlery down onto the plate.

'The fish isn't to your liking?'

She glanced up and met Sebastian's perceptive gaze. 'No, it's fine. I'm just not that hungry.'

He speared a small scallop from his plate and held it temptingly close to her mouth. 'Try this. It's perfection.'

There was an implied intimacy in the gesture, and her eyes widened slightly, then stilled as she was held mesmerised by the sensual warmth apparent in the dark grey eyes of the man seated opposite.

Anneke felt as if she was damned if she took the morsel, and equally damned if she didn't.

'It's easy,' Sebastian said gently. 'Just open your mouth.'

She hesitated another second, then leant forward and took the scallop from his fork with her teeth.

Act, a tiny voice prompted. 'Superb texture,' she commented, and glimpsed the latent humour apparent.

'More?' The query was a soft, sensual drawl, and she shook her head as she reached for her glass.

What was the matter with her? Even the champagne tasted different.

The waiter appeared and removed both plates, queried their preference for tea or coffee.

'Tea—Earl Grey,' Anneke qualified, while Sebastian chose black coffee.

There was music, and a small dance floor, with two couples moving together as a slow ballad emitted from strategically placed speakers.

'Dance with me.'

She looked at him carefully, and knew she should refuse. There was something evident in his expression she couldn't quite define. Sensuality, intoxicating and mesmeric. Bewitching chemistry at its zenith.

Anneke gathered her napkin and placed it on the table,

then stood to her feet and allowed Sebastian to lead her to the dance floor.

He caught her close with natural ease, his steps fluid as he led her slowly round the small square.

She could close her eyes and pretend there was no one else around. Slide her hands up over his shoulders and link them together at his nape. Undo the leather clasp that bound his hair, then thread her fingers at will through its length.

The image remained with her of how he'd looked the first night she'd caught sight of him in her aunt's kitchen. A five o'clock shadow that had deepened into dark stubble, his hair loose and tousled. Even then she'd thought him lethal. *Shameless*, when he'd captured her head and bestowed a plundering kiss.

One ballad led on to another, and it was more than five minutes before the pace changed to something upbeat.

Sebastian led her back to the table. 'More tea?'

'No.' It was after ten. They'd eaten a leisurely meal, enjoyed a dance. There was no reason to linger. 'Would you mind if we leave?'

Sebastian settled the bill, and they walked to the car park. Within minutes the Range Rover eased its way onto the road, then picked up speed as they left the town behind.

Headlights shone twin beams into the encroaching darkness, and Anneke leaned her head back and focused on the road.

At this time of night there wasn't much traffic, and all too soon Sebastian reached the turn-off leading down to both cottages.

Anneke reached for the door-clasp as soon as he switched off the engine.

'Come in and share a drink with me.'

Every nerve in her body screamed an emphatic *no*. 'It's late, and I'm tired.' Did she sound as breathless as she felt? Dear heaven, she hoped not!

He caught hold of her hand and lifted it to his lips. 'You can sleep in tomorrow.'

'Sebastian—'

He stilled her voice by the simple expediency of pressing a hand over her mouth. 'Anneke.' His voice held a teasing quality. 'Are you afraid of me?'

She hesitated a fraction too long. 'No, of course not.'

His smile was warm and infinitely sensual. 'Then come share a coffee with me.'

Ten minutes, she compromised. She'd drink the coffee, then she'd go home.

Shaef greeted them at the door with restrained delight, and sank down at Anneke's feet as she chose the informality of the kitchen in preference to the lounge.

Sebastian shrugged off his jacket and discarded his tie, then he crossed to the sink and filled the coffee-maker with water, ground fresh beans and spooned them into the filter, then depressed the switch. 'Milk or cream?' He crossed to a cupboard and extracted two cups and saucers.

'Milk.'

He opened the refrigerator door, and she saw what looked suspiciously like her *bombe au chocolat*. Beside it was the sponge stuffed with strawberries and cream.

'You should throw them out.'

He shot her an amused glance. 'Not yet. I like to look at them.'

Her voice came out as a strangled sound. 'Why?'

He extracted a carton of milk and closed the refrigera-

tor door. 'Because it reminds me of how much trouble you
went to trying to kill me with indigestion.'

Of course he knew. How could he not?

'I was intrigued to know what you'd dream up to
serve me next.'

The coffeemaker completed its cycle, and Sebastian
took hold of the carafe and filled both cups.

'It was a challenge,' she conceded with a tinge of
humour. She spooned in sugar, stirred, then sipped the
contents. 'I owe you a meal. A decent one,' she qualified.

'An attempt to redeem yourself?'

'I'll go one better,' she said solemnly. 'Give me a menu,
and I'll prepare the food. Do you prefer vegetables or salad?'

'Vegetables. Buttered baby potatoes in their jackets,
asparagus with hollandaise sauce, honeyed carrots.'

'Dessert?'

'You.'

Anneke's eyes flew wide. 'Sorry, I don't decorate body
parts. Suggest something more conventional.'

He replaced his cup, removed hers, then captured her
hands and pulled her towards him. 'Will this do?'

She didn't have a chance to answer. His mouth closed
over hers in a gentle exploration that melted her bones.

Hands moulded her close as he deepened the kiss, and
she opened her mouth to him, slid the tip of her tongue
beneath the hardness of his own, and felt his breath catch.

Anneke wasn't quite ready for the long, sweeping
response as he took her from pleasure to possession, then
staked a claim.

It was all she could do to hang on and ride the storm of
his passion.

No one had kissed her with quite this degree of

hunger, and her whole body throbbed beneath his explosive touch as he began a trail of discovery of each and
every pleasure pulse.

His mouth left hers and sought the vulnerable column
of her throat, the delicate hollow, the edge of her neck,
before slipping low to the soft curve of her breast.

Somehow the zip fastening at the back of her dress
slid free, and the tiny shoestring straps were eased over
each shoulder.

An indistinguishable moan died in her throat as deft
fingers teased a sensitive peak to hardness, then rendered
a similar supplication to its twin.

He took her to the brink between pleasure and pain, then
trailed his mouth down to suckle each tender nub until she
moved restlessly against him.

It wasn't enough, not nearly enough, and a soundless gasp
escaped her lips as one hand slid to the apex between her
thighs, teased the thin silk barrier of her briefs, only to retreat.

Anneke whimpered in protest, then she caught hold of
his head and brought his mouth to her own in fierce possession, testing his control.

She'd thought to delight in his loss of it, but nothing
prepared her for the deep, penetrating invasion that took
hold of her emotions and tossed them high.

Her hands reached for his shoulders and she simply
clung to him until the storm inside began to diminish.
Slowly, ever so slowly, he lightened the kiss until his lips
merely brushed against her own, then he linked his arms
at the base of her spine.

His eyes were dark, so dark they were almost black,
and there was a waiting quality evident beneath the
sensual warmth.

The next move was hers. He was giving her the option to move away from him, say any words by way of excuse, then leave.

If she stayed, it would be because she wanted to, not due to any unfair persuasion on his part.

Indecision warred temporarily as she fought desire with sanity.

How could you know a man for months, a year, *longer*, yet not really know him at all? Then meet another, and see almost at once the heart of the man beneath the many layers fashioned by time and experience?

She could turn away and never know the joy he offered, or the depth of emotion they could share. Yet what was the price she might have to pay?

Sadly, she had the feeling it would be way too high.

'I think I'd better go.'

Sebastian leaned forward and brushed his lips against her forehead. 'I could tell you not to think. Just to feel.'

She lifted her head and met his steady gaze. There was a depth apparent that frightened her. Not out of a sense of threat, but something she was too afraid to define.

'I know.' Her voice came out as a husky whisper. She even managed a shaky smile. 'But you won't.'

He let his arms fall to his sides, and watched the fleeting emotions chase across her expressive features.

Then he watched as she took a backward step, then turned and walked to the door.

'Be ready at nine.'

Her hand froze as she reached for the latch, and she cast him a startled glance over one shoulder.

'Our picnic, remember?' A slow smile spread his mouth. 'I'll organise the food.'

Anneke recovered quickly. 'Nine.' Then she opened the door and closed it quietly behind her.

She'd left a light on inside her aunt's cottage, and it provided a welcoming glow as she crossed the path.

Sleep didn't come easily. Nor did peace of mind. But then she hadn't expected it to.

CHAPTER NINE

ANNEKE woke at dawn, opened one eye, groaned, then rolled over and tried to capture sleep. Two hours would be great, but she'd settle for one.

Ten minutes later she gave up on it and slid out of bed. An early-morning swim, then she'd shower, have breakfast, and package the small Christmas cakes designated as gifts ready to consign to the postal services tomorrow.

She expected to see Sebastian on the beach, but he was nowhere in sight. She ran the length of the cove, then stripped down to her swimsuit for a leisurely swim.

It was almost eight-thirty when Aunt Vivienne rang to report that Elise was progressing so well the doctors were confident she'd go close to full term.

'How are you getting on with Sebastian, Anneke?'

Oh, my, now there was a question! What would her kindly aunt think if Anneke went with total honesty and said she was on the verge of going to bed with him?

'Fine.' That covered a multitude of contingencies.

'Why don't you fly up and join us for Christmas, darling? I know Sebastian is going to Paris, and I don't like to think of you at the cottage alone.'

'That's thoughtful of you,' Anneke declared warmly,

grateful for the option of spending the festive season with family.

It was almost nine when she smoothed a hand down the seam of her designer jeans, then slid nervous fingers along the ribbed hem of the skinny top she'd chosen to wear.

A knock on the door heralded Sebastian's arrival, and she caught hold of her bag, collected her sunglasses, then crossed to open the kitchen door.

Clad in dark blue jeans and a black shirt with the sleeves rolled part-way up each forearm, he looked far too vibrant for any girl's peace of mind.

'Good morning.'

Sunglasses made it impossible for her to detect his expression, and she matched his smile with one of her own.

Sebastian headed the Range Rover north when they reached the open highway.

'Where are we going?'

'The Gold Coast hinterland. Lamington National Park, O'Reilly's.' He spared her a warm glance. 'We'll feed the lorikeets, have lunch, then maybe head down to Surfers Paradise for an hour or two.'

The sun was hot, tempered by a slight breeze, and Anneke was delighted by the friendly lorikeets. Feeding time was something else as the brightly coloured green and red plumed parrots settled on her arms then walked up onto her shoulders. Some even settled on her head, and she laughed when one became over-curious with the band confining her hair. His claws became tangled in the single thick plait, and his squawking brought Sebastian to the rescue.

'Hold still.'

'Believe me, I wouldn't think of doing anything else,' she assured him as he moved in close.

Too close. She was intensely aware of his shirt-clad chest and shoulders only mere inches from her cheek. Clean fabric mingled with the faint musky tones of his aftershave, and played havoc with her senses.

'He won't hurt you,' Sebastian murmured. 'He's just frightened.'

That makes two of us. But it wasn't the parrot she was afraid of.

'There,' Sebastian reassured. 'He's free.' He caught hold of her chin and lifted it. 'His claws didn't scratch you?'

'No.' Her mouth was inches away from his, and she had to control the temptation to reach up and pull his head down to hers.

'Hungry?'

'Yes.' It was true. The mountain air had given her an appetite.

'Come on, then.' He caught hold of her hand and tugged her towards the path leading to where the land cruiser was parked.

Sebastian unlocked the rear door and opened up a portable cooler. *'Voilà.'*

There were fresh steaks, crisp lettuce, fresh fruit, mineral water and a bottle of wine.

'You came prepared.'

His eyes challenged hers. 'Always.'

She doubted if anyone had managed to gain the element of surprise with this man. He was intensely vital, acutely alert, and far too discerning to be caught unawares.

Gas-fired barbecues were positioned at intervals on a grassed area adjacent the car park, and there were tables with fixed umbrellas to shade picnic-makers from the sun.

Sebastian took hold of the cooler. 'Let's grab a niche over there. I'll cook the steaks while you mix the salad.'

They drank a glass of superb Lambrusco with their meal, and washed the fruit down with mineral water.

Anneke rose to her feet and stacked plates and cutlery into a plastic bag ready to place in the cooler.

'Feeling energetic?'

She lifted both shoulders in a light shrugging gesture. 'Not particularly.'

So she hadn't slept much either. After an hour of tossing and turning, he'd pulled on a pair of jeans, booted up the computer and worked until three.

He collected the cooler and stored it in the rear of the Range Rover. 'Then let's head down to the Coast.'

More than an hour later they were seated at one of many tables overlooking the broadwater, savouring cappuccinos. It was a relaxed atmosphere, with numerous people wandering the boardwalk, admiring the many craft moored at the adjacent marina.

The physique, the hair, the dark, attractive features earned Sebastian more than a few covetous glances from the women who passed by their table.

'Oh, my,' Anneke declared, *sotto voce*. 'I think you have made a conquest. That's the second time one particular blonde has walked this way. Perhaps I should go powder my nose and leave a clear field?'

'Do that, and I'll take evasive action,' Sebastian drawled. 'You'll go powder *your* nose?'

He tipped his sunglasses further down his nose and speared her a level look over the rims. 'Kiss you in such a manner there'll be no doubt *you* are my only interest.'

'Wouldn't you be taking an enormous risk?' Anneke

queried sweetly. 'I might push you over the railing into the water.'

'Then we'd both look foolish,' he intoned lazily as he leaned forward and trailed light fingers down her cheek.

Her eyes dilated fractionally at his featherlight touch, and her lips quivered as he traced their fullness with his thumb.

'You've been treading on eggshells all day,' he said gently. 'Waiting for me to pounce?'

She held his gaze. 'I think you have a strategy,' she said with innate honesty. 'I just need to figure out which ploy you intend to use.'

Sebastian laughed, a soft, chuckling sound deep in his throat. He stood to his feet, anchored a ten-dollar bill beneath one saucer, then reached for her hand. 'Come on, let's walk.'

They explored the upmarket shopping complex, then wandered to the wharf market where fresh seafood was sold direct from the fish trawlers.

Anneke examined the prawns, the many varieties of crustaceans. They looked succulent, mouthwatering. 'I promised you dinner.' She shot him a teasing grin. 'Are you willing to trust me?'

'You want to take some of these home?'

'I'm buying,' she insisted as he extracted his wallet. 'I mean it,' she said fiercely.

He lifted both hands in the air. 'OK.'

She chose carefully, with the expertise of a market haggler, selecting, rejecting, until she was satisfied she had the best of the best.

'Let's get this into the cooler and head home.' Her mind was already busy with the preparation she needed to make, the time factor, a mental rundown of salad makings in the refrigerator.

It was almost seven when they reached the cottage. 'Give me an hour,' Anneke said as she extracted the seafood from the cooler. That would give her time to shower and change, and have the food ready on the table.

'I'll bring the wine.'

She managed it with five minutes to spare, and spent four of those minutes wondering if she should change blue jeans for black dress jeans, add blusher and eyeshadow or just stick with lipstick. Perfume?

A knock at the door precluded the necessity for either, and she crossed the kitchen and let him in.

Sebastian took the bottle of chilled white wine to the servery. 'Shall I open this?'

Anneke handed him the corkscrew. 'Please.'

He'd showered, shaved and changed into casual dark trousers and a pale blue shirt. Aunt Vivienne's kitchen wasn't large, and he seemed to fill it.

She extracted two glasses and set them on the table as he eased the cork out from the neck of the bottle.

'Anything I can do to help?'

'It's all done.' Did she sound as nervous as she felt?

He leaned forward and covered her mouth with his own, taking advantage of her surprise by bestowing an erotic tasting. He lingered a few seconds, then lifted his head.

She looked…momentarily startled, and her slight confusion pleased him. 'Shall we eat?'

Oysters mornay, chilli prawns, and crustaceans in their shells, split in half and the flesh coated with a delicate sauce and grilled. Fresh salad greens, and a baguette she'd heated to crunchy perfection in the oven.

'Magnificent,' Sebastian declared, with the pleasure of a man who had eaten well. 'More wine?'

'No,' Anneke refused quickly, and earned a slight smile.

'The need for a clear head?'

She didn't answer, didn't dare. 'I'll make coffee.'

Her movements were mechanical as she set up the coffee-maker, and when she turned to open the cupboard he was right there.

'Sebastian—' His lips settled over the vulnerable hollow at the edge of her neck, and she lost track of whatever it was she'd intended to say.

His mouth was warm, his tongue an erotic instrument as he teased the pulsing cord, savoured it, then used the edge of his teeth to take delicate nips from the sensitive hollows.

She made one last-ditch effort at protest, only to have it die in her throat as he turned her fully into his arms and covered her mouth with his own.

One hand lifted to cup her nape while the other slid down her back and pressed her close against him.

His arousal was a potent force, and she felt her bones begin to melt as liquid fire coursed through her veins. Each sensory nerve-end was heightened to acute awareness, and her body leaned in close to his as he deepened the kiss to an imitation of the sexual act itself.

Anneke wanted to feel his flesh, taste him in a tactile exploration that would drive him wild. Her fingers slid to the opening of his shirt, freed each button, then she trailed butterfly kisses across his chest, tangled her tongue in the whorls of hair, took possession of one male nipple, and suckled.

His body shuddered, then tautened as firm hands clasped hold of her waist, and it was she who cried out as he lifted her onto the servery, then parted her thighs and positioned himself between them.

His eyes were dark and impossibly slumberous as he

tugged her top free from her jeans, then pulled it over her head. The bra clip slipped open with ease, and he slid the straps down her arms and dispensed with the scrap of silk and lace.

Then he buried his face in the valley between her breasts and caressed the soft curves, tormented and teased each roseate peak, then trailed a path down to her navel.

Her jeans were a barrier he dispensed with with ease, tugging them free and dropping them onto the floor.

He kissed her, gently at first, then with an increasingly demanding possession, and when he at last lifted his head she could only look at him in shaken silence.

Sebastian didn't have to ask. The unspoken question was apparent in his stance, the liquid darkness of his eyes, the curve of his mouth.

A slight shudder ran through her body. If she turned away now, she'd never know his touch. And she wanted to, badly.

Not just the physical. She wanted more, much more than that. His heart, his soul. Everything.

Maybe, just maybe, she should take the gamble and run with it. Let emotions take her wherever he led.

A week could be a lifetime. And better to experience a week of heaven than never to experience it at all.

Slowly she reached out and slid her fingers to his nape, where a clip fastened the leather strip that bound his hair. Her eyes never left his as she slipped it free. Then she forked her fingers through the silken river of black, and spread it out so that it flowed onto his shoulders.

It gave him a rakish look that was pure pagan, primitive, and it was a gesture she'd wanted to make ever since she'd first stepped into this kitchen and found him making tea.

His smile was slow and infinitely sensual as he copied

her actions, releasing the thin elastic band at the base of her plait, then threading his fingers through the length of her hair.

It was the expression in his eyes that made her catch her breath and caused her pulse to quicken to a much faster beat.

'I think,' she said shakily, 'you'd better take me out of the kitchen and into the bedroom.'

He played the game, teasing her gently. 'You think so?'

'Otherwise I may never be able to cook or serve food in here again.'

Sebastian laughed. A deep, husky sound that curled into the recesses of her heart. 'Put your arms round my neck.'

Anneke did as she was told, and he kissed her long and deep, then he carried her through to the bedroom, switched on the light, and let her slide down to her feet.

In one easy movement he sought the pocket of his jeans, extracted a slim foil square and slipped it beneath one pillow.

Mesmerised, she stood still as he popped the studs on his jeans, then shucked them off. The thin covering of black silk sheathing his manhood followed, and her eyes widened at the sight of him.

His was a savage beauty. Primal, powerful. A man who could show great strength, even cruelty. Yet there was a tenderness apparent, an acute caring for those who were sufficiently fortunate to win his trust, his love.

Sebastian reached for her, pulling her in close as he tumbled them both down onto the bed. He was hungry for her, wanting, needing to sheath himself in the silken sweetness of woman. Not just any woman. *This* woman.

He needed to show her the difference. Knew, hoped, that she would *know*.

Anneke let her fingers splay over taut muscles at his

shoulders, trailed them to explore his ribcage, then slid down over his flanks to urge him close.

'*Non, mon ange*. We are just beginning.'

He took pleasure in the tasting of her skin, every inch of it, with the pads of his fingers, his lips. And felt her pulse quicken, her breath become erratic and fast.

Her body began to feel like the strings of a finely tuned violin, his touch creating magic that reverberated along each nerve fibre until her whole being *sang* to a tune that had never been played.

The feeling was so intense she could hardly bear it, and her hands became more urgent as she began to plead with him to ease the ache deep within.

He soothed her as she arched against him, caressing the moist heat with a touch that brought her to one explosive climax after another.

It wasn't enough, not nearly enough, and she became a wild wanton in his arms, pliant, bewitching, *his*.

He entered her slowly, allowing the silken tissues to stretch to accommodate him, then he drove forward with one powerful thrust.

Anneke gasped at the level of penetration, absorbed it, then met and matched his rhythm, unable to prevent the soft guttural cries that escaped her lips as he took her higher and higher to the brink, held her there, then caught her when she fell. And kissed the light tears as they trickled from her eyes.

Sebastian curled her close in the circle of his arms, and she dozed for a while, then stirred at the movement of a hand sliding low over one hip.

He was asleep. His breathing hadn't changed. She began a slow, tactile exploration of her own, skimming over warm

HELEN BIANCHIN   103

skin, strong muscle and sinew to his pelvis, lightly examining the faint hollow, the keloid puckering of a surgical scar.

She let her fingers trail up over his ribcage to the dark
smattering of hair on his chest. Hair that was light and
springy, and different in texture from the glossy length he
wore bound at his nape.

More than anything she wanted to explore the angles
and planes of his sculpted features, the chiselled cheekbones, the hard jaw, the sensitive lines of his mouth.

Most of all she wanted to wake him. To feel again the
power of his body as he joined it with hers. The acutely
intense spiral of sensation that mixed pleasure with pain,
then transcended both to rapturous ecstasy.

He'd shown her remarkable *tendresse*. Now she wanted
his passion, unbridled, shameless and primitive.

A hand reached for hers, caught it, and brought it to his
lips. Her heart almost stopped, then quickened to a faster
beat as she raised her head and met a pair of dark eyes
lambent with molten desire.

'You're awake.'

Without a word he kissed each finger in turn, savoured
her palm, then grazed the fragile veins at her wrist.

One slight tug, and she lay sprawled across his chest.

She gained purchase on his shoulders and leant
forward to kiss him, loving the feeling of power as he let
her take control.

The sensual tasting tested his strength, and just when he
thought he could stand it no longer she slid down onto him.
Her movements were deliberately slow as she completed
one erotic circle after another until it drove him wild. His
hands bit into her waist, then splayed over her hips, holding
her still as he drove into her again and again, until it was

she who cried out, and their voices mingled in a mutual expression of wild, untamed passion.

Afterwards, when the spiralling subsided and their breathing returned to normal, he pulled her close and held her there.

Her hair was a mass of tangles from where he'd raked his hands through its length, and he soothed it gently, feeling its texture, the long silken strands that fell in a cloud over her shoulders.

He kissed her, long and deep, then he buried his mouth in the soft hollow of her neck as she slept.

Again and again they turned to each other in the night. As the light fingers of dawn filtered through the windows they rose from the bed and showered, only to return to bed to sleep until the shrill peal of the phone sounded loud in the morning stillness.

Sebastian kissed her briefly as she lifted her head and groaned. 'You'd better answer it, *mon amie*.'

Who could be ringing at this hour? She spared a glance at the bedside clock, and jolted upright. My God, *midday*!

She scrambled out of bed, grabbed the sheet and wrapped it round her naked form, then stumbled as the tucked-in portion stubbornly refused to part from the mattress.

Sebastian chuckled as she swore, and leaned forward to wrench it free.

Anneke raced into the kitchen, lifted the receiver and heard her aunt's anxious tones on the other end of the line.

Thinking quickly on her feet after a long night of loving and very little sleep was difficult. 'I was in the shower.' A necessary untruth, and she shivered as she felt Sebastian's lips nuzzle her neck. When his hands unbound the sheet, there was little she could do except shake her head at him in silent remonstrance.

'Is everything all right, darling?' Aunt Vivienne queried. 'You sound a little…strange.'

His lips sought her breasts, savoured the swollen peaks, then bit gently into the tender softness.

On a strangled note she ended the call, replaced the receiver, then allowed herself to be pulled into his arms.

'You're insatiable,' Anneke said unsteadily as his teeth nipped an earlobe.

'In a minute, I'm going to collect my clothes, go home, and spend what's left of the day at the computer.' His lips trailed to her temple, caressed the fast-beating pulse there, then travelled down to the edge of her mouth. 'I have a deadline to meet before I leave for Paris.'

She turned her mouth to meet his, and wondered if she'd ever be able to survive after he left. 'I'll bring dinner.'

'And stay.'

'Sebastian—'

'Stay, Anneke,' he repeated insistently. 'My bed, or yours. It doesn't matter.'

No, it didn't. To deny him was to deny herself.

CHAPTER TEN

THE days ran into each other, each one seeming more poignant than the last.

Sebastian rescheduled his work pattern from mid-morning to seven in the evening. Dinner was extended by an hour, and the nights were something else as their love-making took on a new dimension.

Anneke told herself she was happy, happier than she'd ever been. And she was. Except the dawn of each new day brought her one day closer to the time she'd have to bid Sebastian goodbye.

Wednesday they drove into Byron Bay township and consigned Sebastian's manuscript to his American agent via courier. Then they celebrated with champagne and dinner at the town's finest restaurant.

'Tomorrow we'll fly down to Sydney.'

Anneke heard the words, but didn't absorb them. 'What did you say?'

Sebastian's smile held a combination of humour and sensual warmth as he repeated the words.

Her heart flipped, then raced to a painful beat. 'We?'

'We,' he gently mocked. 'That will give you time to gather some clothes together, do any necessary shopping, and pack.'

'Pack?'

'You're coming with me to Paris.'

Her mind whirled at the implication, and her stomach began to compete with the erratic beat of her heart. 'What about a passport, visa—'

'Your passport is valid.' His eyes gleamed with humour as her mouth opened, then shut again. 'Vivienne,' he revealed succinctly.

'You've spoken to Aunt Vivienne?'

'I needed to check on your passport, make arrangements for both cottages, Shaef.' He paused for a second. 'And tell her you wouldn't be spending Christmas with her in Cairns.'

Christmas. She'd need to get gifts for his family; she couldn't possibly go empty-handed...

A strangled laugh rose and died in her throat with the realisation she didn't know any details at all, with the exception of his grandmother.

Sebastian caught each fleeting expression and accurately defined every one of them. He reached across the table and caught hold of her hand. 'It'll be fine,' he reassured her. 'Trust me.'

They arrived in Paris mid-morning on a cold, wet, typically grey mid-winter day, tired after a long international flight.

Sebastian collected their hire car, and drove to the gracious old home on Ile Saint-Louis where his grandmother had resided since the day she was born.

A very beautiful home, with exquisite carpets, antique furniture, and *objets d'art* worth a small fortune.

Anneke wasn't sure what she'd expected. Certainly it

hadn't been a very stylish and sprightly woman who could easily pass for fifteen years younger than her eighty years, and whose command of the English language was more than impressive.

'Your rooms are ready. I know you must want to shower, then change and rest.'

'Room, Grandmère,' Sebastian corrected. 'We share.'

'So.'

Anneke couldn't imagine such a little word could convey such meaning.

'Are you not going to introduce me to this young woman you have brought to meet me?'

'Grandmère...Anneke Sorrel.' His arm remained at Anneke's waist. 'Anneke...my grandmother, Madeleine Lanier.'

'Come here and let me look at you.'

'You will frighten her,' Sebastian declared with amusement.

'Indeed.' Madeleine Lanier drew herself up to her full height and glared at her grandson. 'I frighten no one. And if she belongs to you, she belongs to this family.'

A faint smile teased Anneke's lips. 'So you get to pass judgement.'

'She speaks.' Madeleine placed a hand to her heart.

'Indeed she does.' Sebastian leaned forward and gently brushed first one paper-thin cheek, then the other. 'And be warned, she also speaks passable French.'

'I think,' Madeleine declared, 'we should go into the conservatory and take coffee.'

'Tea,' Anneke said gently. 'Earl Grey, if you have it.'

'Has a mind of her own, hmm?'

'Yes, I do.'

'Good. I could not have borne it if Sebastian had brought me an airhead with designs on his money.'

'I do not think Sebastian would have dared do such a thing.'

That earned a quick glance from sharp brown eyes, and the beginnings of a musing smile. 'He has dared many things in his short lifetime. But crossing me is not one of them.' She moved forward and batted her grandson's arm away from Anneke's waist. 'Let her go. We shall get along very well, she and I.'

Madeleine Lanier was a pussycat. An aged, very fiercely loyal lady, who guarded her family with her life. But a pussycat, nonetheless.

Anneke spared Sebastian a mischievous smile, and met his gleaming gaze, saw the faint shrug of resignation that accompanied it.

'You are going to marry her, of course.'

'Of course, Grandmère. I just haven't got around to asking her yet.'

Madeleine stopped in her tracks, turned and directed her grandson a baleful glare. 'And why not?'

Anneke didn't know whether to smile or cry, for there was a very strong possibility jet lag had caused her to imagine the entire conversation.

The glare shifted to Anneke. 'You do *want* to marry Sebastian?'

This was the craziest discourse she'd ever entered into! 'If he asks me, I'll give it some thought.'

'Indeed!'

They took coffee in the conservatory. And tea. With tiny *petits fours* and dainty sandwiches. Then Madeleine shooed them upstairs.

'Your luggage will be in your usual suite, Sebastian. Breakfast,' she declared regally, 'is served at eight. Don't be late.'

The staircase was wide and curved gently upwards in a sweeping arc to the upper floor central landing, from which a wide corridor stretched in both directions.

Sebastian turned to the right and traversed the corridor to its end, then opened the door to an elegant suite with views out over the Seine.

Anneke slipped out of her shoes and crossed to the window. It was drizzling, and what she could see of the city was shrouded in damp mist.

In spring, in summer, it would be clear, the skies a delicate blue, and there would be colour instead of the grey of winter.

Hard, masculine arms closed round her waist and linked together over her stomach, and she leaned back against him.

She felt weary almost beyond belief. She wanted nothing more than a long, hot shower, and a comfortable bed.

'I love you,' Sebastian said gently. 'I planned to ask you to marry me over a candlelit dinner on Christmas Eve, with champagne, a single red rose, the gift of my mother's ring. To introduce you to the family on the day we present and open gifts. Noël.'

His lips touched the vulnerable spot just beneath her ear, and she turned to meet his mouth.

'Yes,' she said simply.

It had been that easy. His arms tightened fractionally. 'No qualifications?'

'Two. We do the Christmas Eve thing, and you bring me back to Paris in the spring.'

His smile stole her heart. 'You're beautiful, *mon ange*. My life.'

Anneke reached up and brought his mouth down to hers. *'Je t'aime, mon amour. Je t'aime.'*

Family, Anneke reflected as she stood within the circle of Sebastian's arms after breakfast on Christmas morning.

The elegant lounge was filled with various aunts and uncles, cousins. And children. Madeleine Lanier's great-grandchildren. Beautifully dressed, exquisitely groomed, and extremely well behaved. Madeleine would not have tolerated it otherwise.

She glanced across the room and met the eyes of the gracious old lady, and smiled.

Everyone together in peace and harmony. Sharing, caring. Hopes and dreams. Gifts and giving.

For Madeleine Lanier, this house, her family, represented a lifetime of memories.

And Anneke had gifted and been given the greatest gift of all.

Love.

There are 24 timeless classics in the Mills & Boon® 100th Birthday Collection

Two of these beautiful stories are out each month. Make sure you collect them all!

If you have missed any of these books, log on to www.millsandboon.co.uk to order your copies online.